Franz S. Ganter

A Romantic Tragedy, in Five Acts

Franz S. Ganter

A Romantic Tragedy, in Five Acts

ISBN/EAN: 9783337048679

Printed in Europe, USA, Canada, Australia, Japan

Cover: Foto ©Andreas Hilbeck / pixelio.de

More available books at **www.hansebooks.com**

Ravenswood.

A Romantic Tragedy,

IN 5 ACTS,

ounded on Scott's Novel of the "Bride of Lammermoor"

AND

RESPECTFULLY DEDICATED

TO THE

SHAKSPEARE CLUB,

BY THE AUTHORS,

F. S. Ganter and George H. Braughn.

NEW ORLEANS:

JOHN W. MADDEN, PRINT. 73 CAMP ST.

1873.

RAVÊNSWOOD.

A Romantic Tragedy,

IN FIVE ACTS.

Founded on Scott's Novel of the Bride of Lammermoor,

AND

RESPECTFULLY DEDICATED

TO THE

SHAKSPEARE CLUB,

By the Authors,

F. S. GANTER and GEORGE H. BRAUGHN.

———

NEW ORLEANS:

JOHN W. MADDEN, PRINT, 73 CAMP ST.

1873.

RAVENSWOOD!

A ROMANTIC TRAGEDY IN FIVE ACTS.

(Founded on Scott's Novel of "The Bride of Lammermoor.")

BY F. S. GANTER AND G. H. BRAUGHN.

Dramatis Personæ.

EDGAR, Master of Ravenswood.
MARQUIS ATHOL, his uncle, after Prime Minister of England
SIR WILLIAM ASHTON, Lord Keeper of Scotland.
COLONEL DOUGLAS ASHTON, his son.
HENRY ASHTON, a boy, also his son.
LORD BUCKLAW.
CAPTAIN CRAIGENGELT, his Parasite.
CALEB, Edgar's Domestic.
BIDE-THE-BENT, a Presbyterian Reverend.
A SCOTCH EPISCOPALIAN CHAPLAIN.
LADY ASHTON, wife of Sir William.
LUCY, their Daughter.
ALICE, their dependent, formerly of the Ravenswoods.
MYSIE, Edgar's Domestic.
    Lords, Bailiffs, Ladies, Attendants, an Apparition, etc.

The Scene is laid in Scotland, during the Reign of Queen Anne.

RAVENSWOOD.

------ • • • ------

ACT I.

SCENE FIRST.—*The shore of the North Sea; Cliffs; a drear No-*
vember morning. On the R. U. side, a Gothic Chapel; in
the rear, Wolf's Crag, from whose portal a funeral pro-
cession with banners, issues to the mournful notes of draped
trumpets. As the head, with the coffin, EDGAR, and the
CHAPLAIN reaches the Chapel's open arch it is met by SIR
ASHTON with BIDE-THE-BENT and BAILIFFS.

ASH. I bid you in the Queen's name : halt ! (*They rest.*)
EDG. Atrocious villain ! Why this sacrilege ?
ASH. That you shall answer—I'll prevent it by
    The substitution of my priest for yours.
EDG. Not till another corpse displaces this.
ASH. Sir Priest, on pain of banishment, were you
    Forbid to minister : avoid this place.
EDG. Stay here in peace. Why tremble, friend ? Are you
    God's Servant, or the slave of man ?
CHAP. Alas ! The Presbytery have denounced
    Me to their creature, to the Keeper here.
BIDE. Beloved Brother, by your leave, I'll clip
    You of this perquisite.
EDG. Demand it of the devil, whom you serve.
ASH. You'll own our Church's funeral rites or none.
EDG. I reck not creeds, but reverence all the gates
    That lead from life to dread eternity.
    (*To* CHAP.) My dying father willed to pass through yours:
    There waits his corpse : Officiate !
ASH. Your duty, bailiffs, bar the threshold there.
EDG. (*draws sword ; attendants follow him.*)
    Upon this theme, I'll cope the world in arms :
    His sainted soul's not safer with our God,
    Than is his sacred relic here with me ;
    Stand back, or I shall end this outrage with
    A bloody stop ! (*They yield ; the coffin is borne in, and rested*
    at the Charnel vault. All enter, uncovered, with swords still
    drawn, save EDGAR, ASHTON *and his party. The Chaplain*
    reads inaudibly from book to " (*aloud*) " *below.*
ASH. You have your way, but you shall rue the day
    You blustered the Lord Keeper down.

EDG. Be you the keeper or the kept of Hell,
    To me you're simply William Ashton. Pray,
    Begone!
ASH. Sir, by your leave, not yet.
EDG. Stay at your peril; in the choleric
    Distempered state, your presence puts me in,
    I'll stand for nothing.
ASH. Ha! you'd not murder me?
EDG.   Sir, did I so
    Forget myself, and God! remember you,
    I would not own the sottish hardihood,
    To dare the presence of my victim's corpse,
    As you my father's.
ASH. Sir, sir—young man, how's this?
EDG.   By Heav'ns! you are
    A feller caitiff than I took you for:
    Your houndish nature prowls around its prey,
    To know it dead for sure, and if it stirs,
    You throttle it for the last. Be satisfied!
    Unlid the coffin; let him see the corpse:
    The deadly grief that you have struck him with
    Is sheeted on his face.
ASH.   O far amiss!
    Not such has been, not such is my intent.
EDG. Sure of his death, you'd raven still his spoils?
    The acquisitions of five hundred years
    Of honorable service to the state were his:
    You, by one tricky turn in politics,
    Have made them yours, and of our house, you left
    Him but yon cradle and this tomb!
ASH. These by the last edict are also mine.
EDG. Insatiate worm! That scorpion sting you spent
    Upon my father's life: it smites not me;
    But I shall take you to a reckoning
    That you shall curse the day you bribed a court.
    This once, depart: Too long I wrong the dead,
    To parley with—you know, sir, what you are.
ASH. I'm spellbound to behold how Death transformed
    The spendthrift Ravenswoods to misers here:
    This Chapel's ancient hoard shall satisfy——
EDG. Ha! now I know you as the wretch you are:
    A man-hyena hunting in the grave!
    I'm not condemned to be the sentinel
    Against your hellish greed: away, by Heavens!
ASH. (*faints*) Save! save! he'll murder me (*Bide supports him*)
EDG.   Murder, after you,
    Is too abhorent to be thought upon.
BIDE. My lord, the Lord's good grace now be your staff.
                (*With Bailiffs leads out* ASHTON.)
EDG. Our Scottish realm's polluted by a ghoul! (*hastens into*
      Chapel.*)
CHAP. (*aloud*) And rest his soul in peace.

EDG. Oh! God, my heart! I will not own it bleeds,
    Until I see the drops! I will not cry
    It breaks, before I hear the crack! Yet, Heaven!
    Your visitation is considerate:
    Knowing I could not bear this sorrow twice,
    You gave me but one father. (*Falls upon and embraces*
        coffin.
                    I have been
    More than begotten—I have lived by you!
CHAP. Yield earth to earth, and dust to dust. (*Movement*
    among attendants.)
EDG. Oh! I would lock your body to my breast,
    Could I stave off your rendering till my own!
    But Nature is too strict a creditor,
    And thus when due doth she recall her loan. (*Lets coffin*
    down into vault. All do the last rites and return into
    the Tower, save EDGAR *and* CALEB.)
CAL. Sad use he had of it! Oh! he shall urge
    High Heaven, where he is, that it requite
    The enemy who wronged him so on earth!
EDG. The culprit's guilt is his dire punishment,
    And he is damned the most who feels no more.
    Let us hence, too; I must see life again.
    'Tis only by the hold of memory,
    Not by their bodies, that we own our dead. (*They issue*
    from Chapel.)
CAL. Alas! you grasp them with such hearted clutch,
    You take from them their hue.
EDG.   Oh! next to death
    Has been my struggle—it is past.
CAL. Breathless we witnessed your forbearance when
    You could have slain him with impunity.
EDG. My heart you cannot see—but looks this hand,
    As it could take a human life?
CAL. (*Grasps it*) God bless you, Master! I do live in you,
    As you did in your sire; continue thus,
    And all who'll know you, shall rejoice in you.
EDG. Stern Death revealed to me this life: it is
    A dreadful ordeal that goads me on
    To action, ever action and no rest!
    And now, by Heavens! I feel that within,
    Which could, methinks, start all the Universe
    Again in motion, if it were to stop!
(*Shouts from Tower*) Long live the noble house of Ravenswood!
CAL. Oh! these gray hairs shall turn to black again
    When I behold it in its former pride.
EDG. Alas! It is in vain for souls like mine
    To cure their private ill, for of the world's
    Inherent and eternal misery
    They rid themselves but in their exit hence.
(*Shouts again*) We'll oust this upstart from the Keepership.
CAL. Ha! now, hear that!

   1*

EDG. I'd speed its echo to the farthest globe,
    If damned iniquity with Ashton fell!
(*Shouts again*) Hail to our next Lord Keeper, Marquis Athol!
EDG. Now there! Have I not said it?
CAL. He is your uncle.
EDG.   But no saint for that.
    Oh! while this craft besotted age prevails,
    The devil changes but the hell remains.
CAL. The more's the pity, that the Lord gave up
    This earth as homestead for the evil one.
EDG.   Ha! there
    You've touched the fundament which I shall sap:
    Yea, were a worse than Satan, he would rule,
    If man acknowleged his dominion,
CAL. Dispute it, sir! Our seers predicted, you
    Would lead the movement that shall change the world.
EDG. Our God forever lets the world go wrong
    For Man's ado to set it right again:
    That change will come, unless mankind prefer
    To prey on one another like the brutes.
    'Tis time for all to get their due on earth:
    None has too little, when none has too much.
CAL. The very blessing we are waiting for,
EDG. Though Evil must continue, it can be
    So vanquished that the good and just prevail,
    And, by His Spirit! Of this blessed earth,
    I'll reassert to God the ownership.
              Enter MARQUIS ATHOL.
ATHOL. Come, Master, you absent yourself too long:
    The host is worthy of his guests. What, though,
    They own the lauds? You have the brains.
EDG. Still let them stay apart, since 'tween the two
    There is such scant affinity.
ATH. There shall be more; come you're too sensitive:
    Your wine makes us forget; we're feasting in
    The cave of winds.
EDG. 'Twill hold me and my father's memory!
ATH. But not your son and yours.
EDG.   Why should it not?
ATH. You'll have no offspring.
EDG.   Prompt me not to taste
    Whereon I've ruminated to my fill.
ATH. Dilate your vision on this tumble-down
    And crazy castle: scan, assess it well—
    Now do you overween, yours is a home,
    To offer to a Lady Ravenswood?
EDG. Itself, not I, shall speak the invitation.
ATH. 'Twill do it with a lofty air—well, well!
    Although a maiden's unstaid fancy course
    Around a cottage, I have yet to hear,
    It settled on a quarry by the sea.
EDG. 'Tis on the earth, the hallowed spot to me,
    And must be to the heart, that locks with mine.

ATH.   I doubt how you would fare; but had your sire
    Proposed so to my sister, you would not be here.
EDG.   But why broach this at such a time?
ATH.   Because this is your time.
EDG.   Sir, you say true;
    It is the altar that requites the grave!
ATH.   Be thou converted to my politics.
EDG.   Oh, sir, thereon I'd have a speech of fire:
    But to what end? 'Twould only scorch my heart!
ATH.   And vex this Age's ear. 'Twere time you learnt,
    Your faith in honesty is heretical.
    But let me be your fortune's priest, and I'll
    Restore to you the Castle Ravenswood.
    I've tripped this Ashton from the Keepership,
    And you shall be my second.
EDG.   Hardly sir:
    Still where I fix, I must be first or none.
ATH.   Be what you will, so I but have the name.
    There's now within a noble company
    Of Marquises and Dukes; the least is made
    An Earl or Count.
EDG.   And still of no account!
    'Tis this proud flesh that ails our body politic.
    But what magician wrought this wondrous change?
ATH.   What other than our annexation?
EDG.   Our
    Annihilation! Scotland! My poor Scotland!
    The damned corruption, you have pampered, broke,
    And Annexation is the Cancer's core!
ATH.   Pray, moderate yourself, and listen.
EDG.   Oh! Scotland's spirit having been undone,
    And prostituted by the vil'st abuse,
    England's, at last, must needs predominate!
    But I'll not be your second, third or last
    In this. If so this union be blest,
    I'll share the general gain; if it be rued,
    I'd not be bettered by my country's worse.
ATH.   Come, do not, like a vulture, ever track
    Corruption by the stench you snuff.
EDG.   But I'll not feed upon it, though the proof
    Be near, how it does make some natures fat.
    When next you have an honest service for
    The State, call me again; till then, farewell. (*Exeunt.*)

SCENE SECOND—*The Saloon in Ravenswood Castle*—SIR ASHTON,
sitting at a table.

ASH.   What boots the father's death, since in the son
    I am relapsed to worse?
               Enter LADY ASHTON.
               Oh! Margaret,
    Since you're the Duchess Sarah's bosom friend,
    You are infected with a recklessness—

LADY. You blunder in your censure,—I from her?
   Sir, were the Duke of Marlborough my spouse,
   Or could a woman carve her own career,
   The English throne would boast another queen.
ASH. She's but in name, what you are here indeed,
   While I'm Vice-Regent of the Scottish realm.
LADY. As you're a vice, 'tis meet I be the regent.
   But why this plaintive mood?
ASH.   Would you had pampered
   My rav'nous appetite for public spoils,
   And never hankered for a private's wealth!
LADY. Our gain from both but whets my taste for more.
ASH. No infant quicker to its mother's breast,
   Than I would nurse me with my country's purse:
   With these deft fingers I could peculate,
   Till they were stiff, and still with smiles and smirks,
   I'd be the safest scoundrel of them all:
   The Commonwealth is not a Ravenswood!
LADY. My vow's fulfilled! He's humbled to his grave.
ASH. You willed the deed; I bear the punishment.
LADY. Wherein, my lord?
ASH. Let Life and Death make answer:
   But now I've got him, I shall aggravate
   His riot at the tomb into rebellion
   Against both Church and State.
LADY.   You overween:
   In him 'twill be imputed to his youth;
   The blame, if any falls upon the Lords.
ASH. He was the leader; they but followed him.
LADY. The worse for him: upon an evil road,
   The best seducer is a first success;
   And this shall be the bait for his destruction.
   But now to touch him, were to spring the trap
   Before the wolf is in.
ASH. Meanwhile he'll range, and I shall be his prey,
   And drag my forfeit life, as if I bore
   My coffin on my back. Still wait, and wait!
   I've damned this patience to the lowest Hell:
   As well bid me go there, and fetch it back,
   As doff me with such tantalizing cheer,
LADY. Make your own comfort then.
ASH.   Oh! Margaret!
   Can you be so indifferent to my fears?
LADY. Beware, my Lord! Though harmless in themselves,
   Imaginary evils breed the real.
ASH. Imaginary! Read the legend there,
   The Ravenswoods' sanguinary creed:
   "I bide my time"! Ha! know you not whereof
   This bull's head is the symbol? It means Death!
LADY. Were it a fox, this Age's type, it were
   A threat indeed! but—pshaw! a bull's dull head?
   Sir, it becomes you well.

ASH.   As does my fear,
    Unless it be, that murder is no more,
    And it be proven that the victims of
    A violent death, have done it on themselves.
LADY.   Old Malise needs must ghost, since in your skull
    He finds his proper haunt, but know, if true,
    That slaughter was three hundred years ago.
ASH.   But yesterday, this Edgar's cousin, Chiesley, slew
    Sir Lockhart in the streets of Edinburgh.
    Since then, I cannot hear a pistol click,
    But cold runs over me; I cannot see
    A knife, but I feel for my sinking heart.
LADY.   Your office warns the assassin to beware.
ASH.   So did the Lord Chief Justice's all in vain—
    This fell, vindictive tribe repeats no place:
    In all there's murder running in the blood,
    And I can have no peace until the race
    Of Ravenswood be rooted from the earth!
    This Edgar is unmarried, has no child,
    And I must strike him, ere he takes a wife,
    Else in his issue, I be cursed again. (*faints*)
LADY.   (*rings*) My Lord, what tricks are these? Though you
        are none,
    Yet seem a man.
ASH.   It is my Chapel fit come back again!
    I feel a qualm, a dread presentiment,
    That I'll soon meet my deadly foe again!
                    Enter SERVANT.
    (*to* SERV.) Go bid my Highlanders to guard the gates,
    And let none in who are not of the house. (*exit* SERV.)
LADY.   There is no cure for him, who needs will ail,
    But I, the sound, shall guard our dignity
    Against a maudlin, craven-hearted fool!   (*Exit*).
ASH.   Alas! not ours a marriage Heaven made!
    My helpmeet's still myself; I'll sound this Edgar;
    If comes the worst, I'll buy my peace of him,
    For till I have't I'm with myself at strife,
    And that's to be with all the world at war—
                    Enter LUCY *with a Lute*.
    Ah! here's my shepherdess of Lammermoor!
LUCY.   Who tends her lambkins in the twilight's mead.
ASH.   Still what you do, is with such gentleness,
    As if it did itself: your presence breathes
    Of innocence and peace. Oh! could you know
    What heaving grief your tuneful spell has lulled!
LUCY.   How gladly I'll resume—
ASH.   Nay, let it, Lucy:
    There is no strain can gladden like yourself,
    For cunningst Art attunes no instrument,
    That's so melodious as the human heart.
    And yours has yet to sound its virgin note.
LUCY.   Sir, when it does, your ear shall hear it first,
    To tell me whether it be true or false.

ASH.   Of that but one can judge : yourself—If 'tis
        Harmonious to your spirit, give to it
        A sweep as boundless as the love of Heaven ;
        But if it jar your nature and your wont,
        Oh! stifle it for 'tis a demon's hiss!
LUCY.   Yet, father, in my text-book I have read,
        That we're best mated in our opposites.
ASH.   A most pernicious treach'rous paradox !
        Is not our conflict with the world enough,
        But to our bosom we must hug the strife ?
        Yea, then the paragon, the demigod
        Becomes a maudlin, craven hearted fool!
LUCY.   Then, like a summer-boat, by drifting ice,
        The heart is crushed in by the freezing stream,
        It rode so gladly in its liquid state.
ASH.   Whence got you that ?
LUCY.   From Observation.
ASH.   True !
        However hot that dreaded place of pain,
        The Hell of married life is killing chill !
LUCY.   I'll treasure your advice, meanwhile I have
        Far better pastime than to think of love.
ASH.   Love is no pastime, Lucy : earthly are
        All other passions; this one is divine,
        For 'tis God's interest and care, that still
        His earth be peopled to the end of time.
LUCY.   I'll think of love with more religious awe :
(grasps his hand) Ah! how now I feel how sacred they, through
            whom
        I got my life ! But 'tis of marriage more
        Than love you speak.
ASH.   A wider charter than
        A child's is yours : wed, Lucy, whom you will,
        A noble or a common, rich or poor,
        So only he be not my enemy.
LUCY.   My father, still in our dislikes we're one.
ASH.   But do not therefor make my likes your own.
        And yet 'tis in your marriage I must find
        The bliss, which in my own I missed!
LUCY.   As I'm your daughter, he shall be your son.
ASH.   My head is for the world, my heart is yours ;
        Though false to all I shall be true to you,
        Who in yourself are such a prize ——
LUCY.   My father!
ASH.   Ah me ! like the returning flood, my plague
        Comes back again ! You oft have spoken of
        An aged servant of the Ravenswoods,
        Named Alice, living still on this estate ?
LUCY.   Oh! sir, she gossips like an oracle,
        And is indeed the living chronicle
        Of Lammermoor. If you would hear her! come,
        I'll take you there.

Ash.   My very wish; let's go,
  And I shall ease me of the woe, you are
  Too young to share, though old enough to hear. (*Exeunt.*)

Scene Third.—*A Glade.   Enter* Edgar *bearing a Gun.*

Edg.   I cannot quell this grief; it will not down,
  For 'tis inherent in the fitful soul
  To rack herself with the reflection of
  What might be, what is not! Yea, ache of loss!
  When first, alone, we venture on the spot
  A dear one hallowed, who's forever gone!
  Blest Memory! still loyal to the dead,
  You've thrust into my passive hands his gun (*touches it*)
  I scarce may use again.—What dreadful roar!
  These native bulls stay savage, though my house
  That bears their stubborn head, is civil now.
  Ha! there he braves defiance to his foe
  And mine: the Keeper as my eyes are true!
  But what revulsion rushes through my breast,
  As Pity strikes my heart's electric cord?
  'Tis not a murd'rous, sacrilegious wretch,
  'Tis but a perilled fellow-man I see!
  He flies! The phrensied bull pursues with tumbling
      bounds;
  He drags a female, and cannot escape!
  Shall I let Retribution swoop him down,
  Or shall I hinder it? Eternal Soul!
  You cannot falter in a moment's test!
  Up weapon, slay the brute, and save the kind! (*Fires
    and rushes out.*)

Scene Fourth.—*The Mermaid's Well.—Re-enter* Edgar, *bear-
    ing Lucy in his arms.*

Edgar.   You are the fairest and the sweetest thing,
  That in this wond'rous world yet rapt my soul.
  Great Heaven who have made this prodigy,
  As 'twere to see your image in her form,
  Now to these drops vouchsafe that quick'ning force
                              (*sprinkles water on her*)
  Which, in your dew, revives the frailest flower!
  Still motionless! My God! can you be dead,
  And I so lifefull cannot give you part!
  She breathes, yet does not stir! Would like the sun
  The earth, I could awake you with a kiss!
  Oh! Heaven, forgive, that I who tremble with
  Creation's kindred thrill, without her leave,
  Thus taste the sweetness of your Eden bliss! (*Kisses
  Nay, hence I'll doubt no more our origin;   her.*)
  My sight's assurance tells, it is divine!
  She opes her eyes, and like a captured fawn,
  She stares on me, imploring for relief.

LUCY. (*Shrieks*) Help, Help! He comes! O save us! Father
    fly!
EDGAR. Fair maiden, do not fear; you are as safe
    And sheltered here, as if you were at home.
LUCY. How is it with me? In what place am I?
    I dreamt I had been gored and trampled on,
    And dying, drew you after to the blest.
    Oh Heavens! You are not my father! speak:
    He is not hurt! Do say, he is not killed?
    Oh let me fly to him! Come, go with me:
    You see how I still tremble—I'm so faint.
EDG. And therefore do not stir, but look on me,
    And be assured as if your father spoke:
    He is as safe, and unhurt as yourself,
    And ran but to the nearest hut for help,
    Of which, thank Providence, there's now no need.
    Rest here, and when he comes, he'll find you well.
LUCY. Now I remember all: the raging brute,
    Our flight, your shot—ah, sir, I know 'twas you—
    The monster's plunge and fall! Oh that was help!
    But for your habit, I would say you dropped
    From Heaven to deliver us from death!
EDG. Or rather say, that Heaven, seeing how
    One of its Angels was beset by ill,
    Has called a son of earth to ward it off.
LUCY. And be you ever blest for answering it!
EDG. Had I not done it, woe were me!
    Had I beheld you, maiden, mangled—dead,
    My desperation would have known but one
    Atonement for my fault, and that had been
    To speed the leaden ball, that felled the brute,
    In your next direst foe—myself,
LUCY. Your speech is kind although your words are dark;
    But I'm still faint and giddy from my fright.
    I shrink and shudder from the stranger man,
    Yet am enchanted by my savior's presence.
EDG. Yea, trust me as you may but one.
LUCY. My trust in you is surety itself.
    But tell me who you are, that I may know
    Who saved my life—who is my second father?
EDG. Still nameless, maiden, let me be to you:
    My patronymic's sound would not accord
    With this celestial moment's harmony.
    It may not grate so harshly on your soul,
    When haply softened by the future's calm.
    But should it still offend, then think, that once
    A stern, forbidden vision crossed your path,
    Whom you may meet again beyond the grave!
    Till then, farewell! I may no longer stay.
LUCY. You shall not leave, before you me teach how
    To pay my life long debt of gratitude,

EDG. Then give to me, what I denied : your name ;
    Which, when I scan my blank of happiness,
    Shall gladden me like tidings from above.
LUCY. That were no token of my heavy debt:
    What is my name if nothing go with it ?
    Yet since you will it, let it go before.
    Of what shall follow after : noble sir,
    My name is Lucy.
EDG.   Lucy, Lucy ? ay !
    The very name I'd wish to call you by :
    It is derived from light. Your name, fair lady,
    Shall henceforth be the light, that shines within,
    While you, the torch, remain unneared, unknown,
    Like yonder sun, which giving, loses naught.
    But now, farewell! My tarrying is not here.
LUCY. Sir, let me pray you : do not doff me thus.
    You see how young I am ; but be assured,
    The more I lack in words, the more's my will.
    Stay 'til my father comes, and he for me,
    Shall say how infinite—Ah, here he is !
        Enter ASHTON ; LUCY *rushes in his arms.*
    My father you are safe, and I'm unharmed !
    Here stands the gentleman, who saved our lives.
ASH. My lord, by what you've done, I'm confident
    You'll pardon my obtrusion now, to own
    You that, for which the name of thanks were but
    A mockery.
EDG.   The issue satisfies
    My will and deed more than a thousand fold.
ASH. Had you, as its disposer, saved my life,
    I'd reverence it as a miracle ;
    But that you snatched me from the brink of death,
    Exceeds the utmost limits of belief.
EDG. What I have done, is it so wonderful ?
    In saving you, I did not hazard aught.
    From neither fire nor flood I rescued you:
    Esteem him rare, who risks his life for life ;
    But I, in helping, did not singe a hair,
    Nor wet a finger.
ASH.   Sir, you hallowed them ;
    Deny me not, to grasp, to kiss this hand (*does so.*)
    Which, to be candid, I did apprehend
    Would once be raised to take, and now, behold !
    It saved my life !
EDG.   I'm still the same unchanged :
    None from himself can alienate his past.
ASH.   What can I say to this,
    More than that mine has been the common fault
    Of rashly judging them we do not know?
EDG. We ever censure under penalty.
ASH. Alas, too true ! But be assured, my debt
    Shall henceforth guage my life's intrinsic worth,
    And by that standard be I blest or doomed !

2

EDG. My lord, the sole requital you can make,
      Is to be ever conscious of this hour,
      For whatsoever cast my future take,
      I'll not stand debtor to an accident.
      Still there's a crying need, that I, Sir Ashton,
      Converse with you.
LUCY. (aside) My father you are much too stiff and cold;
      Come, be to him as cordial and as kind,
      As you are wont to me. You see, he is
      As sensitive as generous.
ASH. Do not defer, but tell me, ere we part,
      How I may show without what is within,
      And yet remain your debtor to my end?
      My will to favor you is infinite,
      And that my means are scarcely less, you know.
EDG. Not this, Lord Keeper, is the proper time:
      Your stirred up feelings billow now too high,
      And I'm as tossed and giddy as yourself;
      Thus I might ask, or you might yield too much.
      Wait till we're fallen to our normal calm;
      Then weigh my grievance by your equity.
ASH. I'll heap my scale until it kick the beam.
      Meanwhile the quittance weighs upon my soul.
      I'll henceforth deem my life ennobled by
      Its being saved by such a man as you.
      Sir, I'm as loth to part, as ere this hour,
      I should have been to meet with you: farewell!
LUCY. (aside) Ah, sir, you are more apt in saving lives,
      Than keeping secrets: how long, do you think,
      Ere I be quit with you in name for name,
      Although your debtor still? But should it chance,
      That in your dark, that light should pale or fall,
      Then, pray, remember, that the torch still burns.
                          LUCY and ASHTON exeunt.
EDG. As I this minute, so great nature felt,
      When first yon sun burst on the universe.   Exit.

ACT II.

SCENE I—*The Tod's Den Inn; enter* BUCKLAW *and* CRAIGEN-
      GELT.

BUCK. Captain, you're welcome back.
CRAIG.   If that were all,
      Mine were indeed a sorry coming-back.
BUCK. I see my blunder: Host! a stoup of wine
      For Captain Craigengelt.
CRAIG.   Now there, again!
                  Enter Host with wine, and exit.
BUCK. I beg your pardon, but what's now your rank?
CRAIG. As various as the countries I have seen:
      From Major on to General in Spain.

BUCK.   Ho! General Craigengelt! (*they drink*)
              It must sound brave——
   In Spanish.
CRAIG.   More kin to fame, than any name
   This pigmy-retching, hero-hungry Age
   Is tooting through its hireling paper trump!
BUCK.   And hence you bluster yours through one—of brass.
CRAIG.   My lord, whom do we serve?
BUCK.   Whom else but the Pretender?
CRAIG.   That's ourselves:
   Are we not all pretenders to the world,
   Which in its turn cheats us? But who can tell
   Where ends the true, and where the false begins.
BUCK.   'Tis even more uncertain than your rank.
CRAIG.   And yet 'tis said, we shall be what we will?
BUCK.   True.
CRAIG.   Well, therefore, since I'm tricked by partial fate,
   I am resolved to be indemnified,
   And pass myself for what I should have been.
BUCK.   Why should you not? You have for comrades all .
   Those chieftains of our great rebellion,
   Who'd still be leaders, had they never led.
   But what credentials did you bear abroad?
CRAIG.   I tapped my sword, and showed how fields were—lost.
BUCK.   (*shakes hands*) A Captain here, and a General when
        abroad,
   A famous, clever fellow everywhere.
   But sir, your martial and heroic air?
CRAIG.   Ha! now you're worth to be a woman.
BUCK.   Why?
CRAIG.   Because they staid convinced, when all the men
   Had nosed me out a mere imposter.
BUCK.   I must confess, it has deceived me too :
   How got you it:
CRAIG.   As from a musk rank company you take
   Its scent; so from the incense Peace distils
   From lucky war, I am so odor charged,
   That were you scented with the fumes from me,
   There's not a dame in Lammermoor, but she
   Would swoon to you.
BUCK.   And do they so to you?
   Come now—your smirk confesses it.
CRAIG.   Let silence lock the hopeful lover's lips.
BUCK.   He is a robber, not a conqueror
   Who hides his booty.
CRAIG.   Well—to tell is not to share :
   Lady Aston's dainty organ scented it,
   And it was sweet to her.
BUCK.   Whereon she sneezed—True, rumors will conflict;
   Yet as I read my proof—of two reports
   About a woman—I'll believe the worse.
CRAIG.   Now, by your manhood, you'd not intimate—

BUCK.   I name no one, nor would I scandalize,
   Though truly, there is many a dame who knows,
   That her repute is better than herself.
CRAIG.   Well, let them know't; but fingers on your lips:
   When I rehearsed to her a certain tale,
   She scowled and fiercely flashed her eyes, as, like
   A restiff tigress, she would break her bonds.
BUCK.   I too am fettered where I would be loose:
   Why should we stinted bachelors not glean
   The field, a married Dives does not care
   To harvest? Let us hear your tale.
CRAIG.   That golden Age, long prayed for, and in vain,
   But even now prevails where I have been:
   There they love well, who never loved before,
   And they who ever loved, love still the more.
BUCK.   A rare, pecular region that for hearts!
CRAIG.   A most prolific, love producing clime,
   Where flock the lonely dowagers, when by
   Their pulse they feel their Indian summer's heat;
   But more than matrons', widows' or of maids,
   It is the married women's Paradise,
   When they would shun the scandal of divorce:
   There by their left hand, they can wed again.
BUCK.   I've heard of men who took a dozen wives
   By morganitic form, but that a woman
   Should wed more husbands to her first? It is
   A most desirable abomination!
CRAIG.   When I return, like the good book, I'll say
   To you: "Sell all thou hast, and follow me"
   Where your forerunner is my good report.
BUCK.   Wherein?
CRAIG.   What else but this? (*points to sword*) The masters
   The continent, the Monsieur Fondre Feus,
   The Meinherr Sauhiebs and the Senor Pocopocs
   Are but an awkward squad compared to you.
   Are you in practice?
BUCK.   I hold my own, or rather am improved.
CRAIG.   'Tis well, for by that fence you scale your goal.
BUCK.   Hold in! 'Tis Ravenswood: be politic.
             Enter EDGAR.
   Lord Edgar, you are pale.
EDG.   My hopes are ashy; you're from Edingburgh?
BUCK.   Old Scotland is no more.
EDG.   What? Can a nation die, and Nature make
   No sign?
BUCK.   There were no tokens save the ones we got.
EDG.   Why sir: were it a pensioned dog you finished,
   The telling of it should affect you more.
BUCK.   No death is near to me, except my own,
   And that, thank Heaven! I'll not live to mourn.
EDG.   Still have I prayed against a nation's fall,
   And now the first I hear of, is my own!
   Even thus a people die: Oh Scotland! on
   Your moors I'll own my sorrow, but not here.

BUCK. I too regret our country died—so poor,
    Else we had got more bonus for our votes.
EDG. Sir, have no care: the roster of the damned
    In Hell includes you all.
BUCK.   To solace you
    We kept our country's name.
EDG.   Her epitaph!
    Oh honesty! you're still as hard a road,
    As when you first were trod!
    Is it for this you are our country's lords:
    To sell it as no savage would his tribe?
BUCK. Pshaw! leave your patriotism to the mob:
    The thrifty class desire this Union.
EDG. O Scotland! what you are therein, you'll know,
    But never what you would have been without!
BUCK. Yourself, the greatest stickler have confessed,
    The English genius overcame the Scotch?
EDG. I know whereof I spoke: I never willed
    Our Scottish nation should drop from the list.
BUCK. She's now great England's mate, who leads this Age.
EDG. But not the future, for her guide's not true.
    Full soon she will decline, and in her fall
    Our Scotland's is involved.
BUCK.   Prevent it then.
EDG. My country! had you but maintained your own
    Integrity, your mission would have proved
    What Greece's, Rome's, yea even Palestine's
    Have never been to Man, for in your frame
    I would have breathed such a flame, you would
    Have been the beacon of the world!
BUCK. Ah sir, for that our Scotland were too poor.
EDG. The spirit's only to the spirit known:
    Where it prevails, a waste Metropolis
    Springs grander than before, but where it lacks,
    A Paradise falls to a wilderness.—
    But since my country lets me be no Scot,
    The world holds out to me to be a man!
CRAIG. And what a man! Madame de Maintenon
    Declared the Master's would eclipse the fame
    Of Marlborough, whose horoscope she set.
EDG Sir, whom have I the honor?
CRAIG. I'm General Craigengelt—in Spain.
EDG. Your wits are very Spanish.
BUCK. Come, head a rise in these united realms,
    And we'll dethrone this chessboard queen, this Anne
    For our Pretender: you shall be his next.
EDG. My lead's in education, not in war:
    It is the pen that tills, the sword but reaps.
CRAIG. Pray, Bucklaw, do not vex the Master more
    With politics: his gallantry prefers
    The saving of a miss's life, to States,
    Especially, if she's the Keeper's daughter.

2*

EDG. I see our converse has been at its best,
    And so, let's break it off—farewell.   (*starts.*)
CRAIG. (*aside*) Detain him yet, without him we shall fail.
BUCK. I hope the Master still will deem us friends.
EDG. Sir, that I may not, for to me that name
    Is hallowed : when I've said, "you are my friend,"
    In weal or in distress, I dare for him
    The farthest lengths as for myself; but for
    This brotherhood, our casual intercourse
    Is much too base.
CRAIG. (*aside*) Browbeat him sir: depend upon your fence.
BUCK. Then let me tell the Master, never Man
    Shall slight my friendship with impunity,
    Nor injure me by deed, by word or look,
    But he must render strait account thereof.
EDG. Into what viper's nest have I trod here ?
    But I divined you right: your conduct proves,
    You are not suited for my company.
BUCK. By Heavens ! Master, know that we are peers !
EDG. No truly we are not: you are a lord,
    While I am simply Edgar Ravenswood !
BUCK. I beg your pardon then : I had forgot
    That I too called you lord—by courtesy.
EDG. Hence call me what you will: it matters not.
BUCK. Then by the law's 'taint : Traitor Ravenswood !
EDG. Of all the epithets you might bestow,
    A traitor's were the least ; but I am none.
BUCK. Sir, you inherited your father's shame,
    And was he not the most redoubtable
    Of rebel traitor chiefs, in that most damned,
    Most wicked, causeless, foul rebellion,
    That ever from its drowsy slumbers waked
    A christian world ?
EDG.   Sir, traitor he was none,
    For he betrayed no trust nor friend, but first
    Declared his party, ere he drew his sword.
BUCK. Was he not steeped in gore and treason to his ears ?
EDG. An unsuccessful revolution 'gainst
    A wrong, corrupt, perverted government
    May be an error, whose worst punishment
    Is its own failure, but it is no crime.
BUCK. No crime ? Our country had declared it so.
EDG. And by so doing, has undone herself:
    When she did brand as crime what is no crime,
    She gave her license to that wickedness,
    Which bred the scoundrels, who have wrought her fall.
BUCK. But I was loyal : that atones for all.
EDG. That you traduce my father and myself,
    I do not reck of you, who parrot like,
    At random, mouth the phrases you are taught.
BUCK. Come sir, your finest airs and wisest words
    Can never bend or break our quarrel's point.
EDG. I told you I will have no feud with you,
    So do not force it on.

BUCK. First draw, and then depart to where you may.
CRAIG. S'blood if it comes to steel, I'll steal away.　　　　*Exit.*
EDG. Bar not my way; pray, let me hence, in peace.
BUCK. Then with your very sword, I'll beat you hence.
　　　　　　　　　　　　　　　(*About to grasp it.*)
EDG. Rash fool, forbear! You, passion's basest slave,
　　To what damnation would you drag us both?
BUCK. Well, sir, defend yourself!　　(*draws.*)
EDG.　　　　　　　　Make sure I shall.　　(*draws also.*)
(*At guard.*)　What boots to crush but one of Hydra's heads?
　　Would all her damned corruptionists had stood
　　Within my good arm's reach, then would I have
　　A country yet; I would have served them thus!
　　　(*They fight; Bucklaw's sword flies from his grasp, and he falls
　　　on his knee.*)
BUCK. The devil arms you, Ravenswood: you strike
　　As if you meant my sword shall hit the moon.
　　You know the bloody code of Scottish feuds;
　　Then follow suit, and upward send my soul!
EDG. Not Ætna could do that: though hellward bound,
　　I'll not let you degrade my image: rise.
BUCK. (*rises.*) You won the throw; come draw the stakes:
　　my life.
EDG. Ill counselled trifler, keep, to mend it if you can.
BUCK. I'll try to do it; But Lord Ravenswood,
　　You strike like Vulcan in his crazy rage:
　　Your blow benumbed me like a thunderbolt.
EDG. You know me not, else you would have bewared:
　　There is in me a power slow to move;
　　But once evoked, it grapples but to crush.
BUCK. Egad, I'll shift me hence beyond its reach.
　　Let us be reconciled.
EDG. As we have been, so shall we still remain:
　　I love you none the better after this,
　　Than ere I fought with you.
BUCK.　　　　　　Sir, I recant.
EDG. No, sing it still; I am a rebel to
　　The government, the system and the creed
　　That pampers villains and slights honest men.
　　　　　　Enter HOST, *who whispers to* BUCKLAW.
BUCK. I am tracked hither by the hounds of law:
　　If not my friend, then be my savior still,
　　Or else this life, which you presented me,
　　Is but a forfeit gift: sir, I implore—
EDG. The gate of Wolf's Crag opens to distress
　　But to your plots let me be stranger still.
BUCK. My peril tears me hence, and I can give
　　You only broken thanks, but it is here (*points to his breast*).
　　　　　　　　　　　　　　Exit with HOST.

EDG. How true this restless monitor within
　　Approves himself! My quick elastic soul,
　　That with its proper wings still upward flies,
　　Can be dragged down but by the stranger ties;
　　And therefore let my soul be Argus eyed,
　　That in her choice of mates she still be right!　　*Exit.*

SCENE 11—*The Hall in Wolf's Crag; A Thunderstorm.*
CALEB *and* MYSIE.

CAL. Pray, Mysie, pray no more to leave this earth:
       The Master says, it is no vale of tears.
MYS. The tongue's unblest that taught it me as one,
       For it has made an autumn of my spring.
CAL. Thus fate tricks women: you regret you had
       Your low'ring season; some repine that in
       Their May of life they did not have their fall.
MYS. Yet we all pray to go to Heaven.
CAL. For that pray neither, since they'll have up there
       Another civil war: best tarry here
       Till it be over. Ha! do you not hear
       How for artillery practice they have made
       A target of this castle? Splash! there goes
       Another capstone from the battlements.
MYS. Alas! my hopes are not so much for Heaven,
       As that the Master here be better housed
       Than in this tower, only fit for owls.
CAL. (*taps her shoulder*) That prayer's heeded: the celestial
                                                  host
       Are even now at levelling down its walls,
       And who can tell, but that to-morrow night,
       The Legion devils with their pioneers
       Will raise a fortress here, of adamant,
       To spite their heavenly adversaries? Whereby
       The Master gets a castle gratis? Eh?
MYS. You're merry, Caleb, but I do not know:
       I am as wanted to this castle as
       The oyster to its shell.
CAL. And when 'tis opened, what a savory,
       Delicious morsel we shall see in you!
MYS. To see, you rogue, is not to taste (*taps his mouth.*)
CAL.   When out of season.
       Well, when he brings this Keeper thief to terms
       And gets his due, we too shall have our own.
MYS. How so?
CAL. Why, get each other—we shall marry.
MYS.   Come,
       So long has been your term of grace, you're past
       All grace with me.
CAL. Ha! you'd be surer, had I left a pledge
       Of my affection; but you showed so oft
       We were, that I forgot we were not wed.
MYS. You men are most preposterous animals:
       Unmarried, you belie your single state,
       And wedded, you confound your marriage bond.
CAL. Well I'll repair my fault.
MYS. How know you, marriage then be still allowed?
CAL. If not, we needs must do what is forbidden,
       For Man unmated, is but half a man,
       And joys unshared, are but the dregs of bliss.

MYS. Yet, you repent your former marriage !
CAL. But tell me, have you not perceived
　　By its reflection in the mirror of
　　Our own transparent love, that Edgar too
　　Has been transformed like me ? That he too is
　　Uxu—uxurious—that he's in love ?
MYS. Not he indeed! he loves the world too much
　　To fix his heart on one particular thing.
CAL. Not if he'd find his mate ?
MYS. 　　　　　　　　　No. rather say,
　　If she find him, for she who'll be his wife
　　Must meet him half the way.
CAL. Then he'll die single, for the world gives proof,
　　So long as woman's heart shall yield and rue,
　　Dissembling wooers win more than the true.
　　But hark! He's coming: quick look to the fire. *Exit* MYSIE.
　　　　Enter EDGAR ; *throws off cloak, and steps to window.*
EDG. O Heaven! thus you fan my fev'rish soul;
　　When Man offends me, Nature soothes me ever:
　　Be she in deigning or in frowning mood,
　　I don't intrude—am not too much, with her.
　　Hand me a chair—Another rumbling clap !
　　How through this breast the thunder leaps and rolls,
　　And quickens me to front Eternity !
CAL. Here is a chair; pray, Master, rest.
EDG. When you behold the like of this, then know,
　　It is the tempest of the Ravenswood !
　　Bid Mysie to prepare a bit of lunch. 　　*Exit* CALEB.
　　I'll hence again, for in a storm like this,
　　I and my ancestors hold conference.
　　　　Re-enter CALEB, *with Lunch.*
CAL. There's knocking at the gate.
EDG. 　　　　　　　　Go. open it.
CAL. All of the house are in.
　　EDG. (*about to rise.*) Nay, if you fear—
CAL. It is not that; but sir, I would not have
　　A stranger spread abroad what here he's seen.
EDG. Tush, your old whims about our humbleness !
　　What we enjoy, we own ; and by that right
　　The universe is mine ; attend the gate. 　　*Exit* CALEB.
　　How excellent the world's duplicity !
　　They will profess a God born in a crib,
　　And yet deny the man who lives in one !
　　　　(*Re-enter* CALEB *with* ASHTON *and* LUCY, *both hooded.*)
CAL. (*to Ash.*) You have before you Master Ravenswood.
　　(*to Edg.*) The strangers say, they'll introduce them-
　　　　　　selves. 　　*Exit.*
EDG. Be welcome hither, whether friend or foe.
ASH. We have been overtaken—
EDG. 　　　　　　　　Pray, forbear ;
　　The elements have been more eloquent
　　In your excuse than tongue could be, unless
　　An angel tell it in this huntress' guise.

ASH. Yet, sooth, I had designed this interview,
    Precipitated haply by the storm.
EDG. Precipitated? Then, since unprepared,
    Retain your mask, and seem you still unknown;
    Or bare your visage: do, as suits you best,
    I'll know you as none other than my guest.
ASH. Sir, to assure you, that I visit here,
    Not with one forward, and one backward foot,
    I'll doff this habit of the chase (*unhoods himself.*)
    Thus let the savior confront the saved.
EDG. 'Tis not my sight reminds me there were two,
    (*to Lucy*) Eor by the grateful air you brought with you,
    I had descried the progeny of Heaven.
ASH. Lucy, compose yourself; take off your hood.
EDG. Nay, urge it not against her bashfulness:
    What need we see the sun to be assured,
    It is its beam that cheers and quickens us?
    What need we look upon the violet,
    To know, it is its scent that raptures us?
    Fain would I do those gentle offices,
    Whose wont, from long disease, I have so much
    Outgrown, that in my own house I'm a guest.
        Enter MYSIE.
    (*to Mysie*) Be you the Luna to attend this sun,
    For by her borrowed light you hence shall shine.
LUCY. (*to Edg.*) Thus by the kind reflection of the moon
    You still will have the vanished sun to shine.
    But in my almanac, 'tis now eclipse:
    So pray you, Moon, to hide the sun awhile.
MYS. (*to Lucy*) Were but our castle not so poor!
LUCY. 'Twould bankrupt Croesus, did he purchase it
    At my appraisement.
MYS. I am so glad it pleases you.
LUCY.   So much
    I would be put in some relationship:
    Could you not part your time 'tween here and me?
MYS. If I knew how.
LUCY   Come, we shall find a way.
           Exeunt LUCY, MYSIE *and* ASHTON.
EDG. Were this a dream, it yet would be a bliss
    Unparagoned by aught my spirit knows;
    But as this visit is a living fact,
    It hits beyond my fancy's highest dare.
        Re-enter CALEB.
    This room has held, this castle holds her yet!
CAL. It does! It does! Master, they are secure:
    I've locked the castle's gate: you are well served.
EDG. Your self-praise makes me doubt.
CAL.   It's all the same:
    A smuggling brig lies in Wolf's Haven, cleared
    For France. The skipper will, for fifty pounds,
    Abduct the Keeper to a hostile port,

Whence for his ransom he shall render back
All the estates he robbed your father of.
Master!—Alas, he hears, but does not heed!

EDG. You jar a discord in the harmony,
Now thrilling through my soul.

CAL. (*aside*)   That harmony!
Pray God, he be not in love!
(*aloud*) Seize him and see how quick he will disgorge,
Ay, and give you that harmony to boot.

EDG. You found my key, but do not let it sound :
Like broken flowers, some conceptions lose
The savor when expressed. But, since you will,
Be turnkey still : go, and unlock the gates.

CAL. O Sir, the devil must be fought with fire.

EDG. Do not believe it, for the devil still
Has most of it ; yea, and can ply it best
Remember this, and what you've done, undo. *Exit* CALEB.
I am alone and yearn for her return,
If but to re-assure me, she is here.

Re-enter ASHTON.

ASH. If now the Master deigns, we shall resume
Where, at the Mermaid's Well, we made a pause.

EDG. My Lord, as then the time, so now the place
Is all unsuited for that conference.

ASH. Pray, fit it then, for in my soul I vowed,
That this day's sun should not go down, without
It saw me fully reconciled with you.

EDG. Your wish is echoed in my heart, but here
It cannot be : you are my visitor,
And still the guest must feel the host's duress,
However hospitable he may be.

ASH. It is as far from me to feel, as 'tis
For you to exercise that influence.
Ask what you will, I yield, for to my bond
You have my signature in blank.

EDG. Alas! what reparation can you make
To my wronged father? Speak it softly, sir!
There where you stand, he breathed forth his last :
It was the direst curse upon his foe,
The air of Heaven ever bore aloft.
Do what you may : could you give thousand worlds,
No benefit accrues to him : he's dead !

ASH. It can! It will! for still he lives in you,
Or rather, as you were my savior,
Be I, instead your father : be my son! (*gives hand.*)

EDG. My lord, you venture on the dearest tie,
That this side Heaven is vouchsafed to Man.
If it comes from your heart, 'twill twine to mine
With such a firm, tenacious ligament,
As not the tear of even death shall rend.
But if your proffer is but tongue begot,
It had been better for us both, that I
Had then withheld my arm, and that dumb brute
Had tossed your soul into eternity !

ASH. Sir, if I falter, if I fail in this,
   Be then the retribution visited,
   Not on myself alone, but all my house,
   Whereof, dear Master, henceforth you are one.
   Command, dispose of me, and all of mine;
   This only once, let me prevail with you:
   Return with us to Castle Ravenswood.
EDG. That were to turn from all my cherished Past!
   And yet 'tis bootless to continue it:
   If Nature had designed us to go back,
   Instead of forward, these our eyes and feet
   Were posted in our rear, not in our front.
ASH. Sir, to a third this will be trebble joy:
   I'll tell my Lucy; we shall hence at once.   *Exit.*
          Re-enter CALEB.
CAL. Oh Master, do not go! Remember now
   That prophecy, the Highland minstrel sung:
   " When its last Lord to Ravenswood shall ride,
   " And claim a dying maiden as his bride,
   "Then in his father's hall his blood shall run,
   " And there his race shall end as it begun.
EDG. Why, Caleb. did I wish a prophecy,
   That one would fit my heart: it gives my blood
   More than I ask: the Castle Ravenswood;
   And as to owning of a dying maid?
   Great Nature wills, a maid die in the bride.
CAL. But, Master, tell me, is your harmony
   Not from,—does she not play? (mimics as on piano)
EDG.   O Man she sweeps
   The chords, that sound the music of the spheres!
CAL. Then Master, never mind the prophecy:
   If it be that she plays, you must be safe,
   She is a winsome lassie—and here, she gave me these.
        (*slips some gold pieces into his hand*)
EDG. But surely not to give to me again?
CAL. Up there are servants too: civility
   Comes then but freely when 'tis bought.
EDG. I carry money with me.
CAL. But this already used to give away.
EDG. Then be it so; I rather spend your cash
   Than more words now. Good Caleb, fare you well.   *Exit.*
CAL. He's gone, and down the stairs with arrow flight
   He's after her. Thus woman shall maintain
   Dominion over man: the last of us
   Will be as much an Adam as the first.   *Exit.*

ACT III.

SCENE I—*Before Alice's Hut; Alice seated beneath a weeping birch.*
    Enter to her EDGAR, LUCY *and* HENRY.

ALICE. (*to Lucy*) But now a fawn stole by: it did not tread
   So light as you my child. You are, I trow,
   Elated by some happy news?

LUCY.   I am indeed, as were I borne on wings—
    This festal spring, and oh!—To witness all
    How fain I'd let you have my sight!
ALICE.   I see, my Lucy, with your very eyes.
LUCY.   Dear Alice, sooth; you look through memory
    Still with the eyes of youth.
ALICE.   I'd own no other,
    For then the world is at its best. But tell,
    Who comes with you? It is as if he stepped
    Across its threshold from the Past! I'm sure
    He's not your father.
LUCY.   Why not he?
ALICE.   Ah, that peculiar, haughty step I've heard
    Was owned by only one, but he is dead!
    Yea, were it not too strange, I would affirm,
    It is the son of Allan Ravenswood!
EDG.   My cherished nurse! It is your heart, not ear,
    That has thus wonderfully recognized
    Your foster child: I'm Edgar Ravenswood.
ALICE.   I've parted with amazement long ago,
    But now, despite your own avowal and
    My cunning ear, I'll not believe—come, let
    This knowing hand of old, pass o'er your face.
                    (Edgar sits beside her.)
    It is too true! these lofty lines of pride
    Agree well with the bold and soulful tone.
    And yet! my only hope, to meet with you,
    Is broken by the grief to meet you here.
EDG.   *(rises)* Where else? I must to you; you will not come
      to me.
ALICE.   Remember Edgar, oh, remember well
    The oath we all have taken: they who left
    Shall not return, and they who staid, shall not
    Depart, till Castle Ravenswood has been
    Restored to him, whose name it bears.
EDG.   I've broken with the Past and all its hate.
ALICE.   You've broken with your oath, whereof you brought
    The scourge along, and yet you know it not!
LUCY.   The Master, Alice, is my father's guest!
ALICE.   Indeed! And is he so? Your father's guest!
    (to herself) Oh, forfeit Lucy! Fated Edgar: Both fore-
      doomed!
HENRY.   Come, Master, see! I found an owlet's nest!
                    (draws Edgar aside.)
LUCY.   I charge you, Alice, in this terrible strain,
    Do not proceed! or if you will, then choose
    Another time. Oh, do not interpose!
    You would not rob me him, my only one?
ALICE.   Fond child, you do not own him yet.
LUCY.   Oh, help me win him! Now or never prove,
    As what I've cherished you!
ALICE.   I surely do it—by denying you.
LUCY.   Alice, my God! How I have been deceived!

  3

ALICE. (*taking her hand*) No child: now most of all, I'm true
    to you.
LUCY. Oh, then be merciful!
ALICE.   I shall be so,
Wherefore let me have private speech with him.
LUCY. What? Would you pass upon my life and death,
    And I not present even?
ALICE. Do you not trust him?
LUCY. Oh, ask it of the blest, if they trust God!
ALICE. Then be content: from him you'll take my words
    More kindly then from me.
LUCY. Alas! you said, I came here like a fawn;
    Now, like a death-struck hind, I make away.
ALICE. Be but a little patient.
LUCY. You were so reverent, I looked on you,
    As one already minist'ring in Heaven,
    And now?—Oh God!
ALICE. You'll learn, that I have done its office.
LUCY. No, never, Alice, if you draw not back
    This fatal arrow! Henry, come; we'll leave
    The Master here; she'd speak with him alone.
    (*to Edg.*) Upon our way, we'll take a rest beside
    The Mermaid's Well; (*aside*) beware, lest she estrange—
    I mean—bewitch your soul.   *Exit with* HENRY.
EDG. (*looking after Lucy.*) What here remains, is but an
    empty vase:
My life and being go along with you!
ALICE. Recall those words, before you learn their weight:
    They are your destiny!
EDG.   If they were not
I'd not have spoken them.
ALICE.   First know, then own.
EDG. Then give me your intelligence.
ALICE. A tale like mine should bear its proper voice:
    'Tis not for tongue to tell.
EDG.   Still give it speech:
Whate'er you harbor, let it leap from you
As 'twere the gladsome thunder from the clouds.
But do not utter what you have to say,
Like robbers do their booty; even now
You muttered, fated, and I know not what,
As you named me.
ALICE. And Lucy!
EDG. Why do you couple us so darkly!
ALICE.   For
One dread fatality enshrouds you both.
EDG. Wherefore, and by whose fault?
ALICE. The fault of many, but your own the most.
EDG. In what have I transgressed?
ALICE. Even wherein you thought to bless yourself:
    In saving Ashton.
EDG. Have Heav'n and Hell exchanged their places?
ALICE. This earth stands to them as it ever did.

EDG. Then is the saving of a human life
    No trespass ?
ALICE. The object makes it one.
EDG. With you, but not with Heaven.
ALICE. Would 'twere with me, and not with Heaven, whose
    Dread vengeance you have intercepted !
EDG. Think you, I'd couple God with vengeance ?
ALICE. Then call it retribution, which shall live
    So long as men transgress, and that's forever.
EDG. I thwarted but an accident.
ALICE. An accident ? The guise for God's design !
    The score of years I dwell here, Ashton came
    Not near, save once : to learn your parts from me.
    He left in dreadful consciousness, that he
    Must yield his forfeit life——
EDG. When I appeared, to save the culprit, and
    To slay his destined executioner——
ALICE. Whereby you doomed yourself his fellow victim !'
EDG. I too saved Lucy ; speak : was that a trespass too ?
ALICE. It was : her death had been the happier.
EDG. So had been mine.
ALICE. Then Heaven help you both !
EDG. I charge you, Alice, to be plain with me :
    Disclose the worst and I will cope a worse.
    Within my bosom springs such potent bliss,
    As turns, whate'er you pour, into itself.
    Is it some taint in her you'd warn against ?
ALICE. Have you seen aught amiss ?
EDG. Sooth, Alice, when my heart rose to my eyes
    They looked indeed for them : they were not there.
    But oh ! full soon I found, 'twas in her soul
    She bore her kindred's wings.
ALICE. Yea, suns may have their spots, but she has none.
EDG. You draw a flaming iron 'cross my heart !
    Then why do you so dreadly warn me back ?
    Do I love unrequited ?
ALICE. What ? You, all eyes and ears have not construed
    The longing, yielding converse of a maiden's heart ?
EDG. In love, I take no hint : it is too dread,
    Too hallowed to my soul.
ALICE. Know then, she loves you so, had she not been,
    She were an angel now.
EDG. Unsay those words, or say them once again !
ALICE. Fond Man, if 'twere not true, my saying it
    A thousand times, would never make it so.
EDG. Has she confessed it ?
ALICE. I might say so, but that she'll do to you.
EDG. Enough ! That seals my fate ! Why stay I here,
    Away from her ?
ALICE. Yet tarry, Edgar.
EDG.   What's to hinder us ?
ALICE. The worst of all, and that you have to learn.
EDG. You heard from Lucy, I'm her father's guest.

ALICE.   So have been many, but yet they never got
    To be his sons-in-law.
EDG.   But none of them
    Did he affiliate as he did me.
ALICE.   Alas! trust not his tongue: it buds profuse,
    But bears no fruit.
EDG.   Remember, now the slip of gratitude
    Is grafted on his soul.
ALICE.   Where it will die:
    His heart is shifting like the desert's sand.
EDG.   You damn him from report, as erst I did.
ALICE.   Woe be to you, when you shall know him as
    He knows himself.
EDG.   Concede, his love is sham—his fear is true.
ALICE.   Grant more: that he redeem what to your hope
    He pledged, yet then——
EDG.   Then, Alice, I repeat:
    What hinders us?
ALICE.   Oh! hear it since you must:
    The dog-star in yon lovers' firmament
    Is Lady Ashton.
EDG.   Oh! that malignant Earth must interpose
    Between them, Heaven has together fit!
ALICE.   'Tis she, who wrought the ruin of your house.
EDG.   Alas! my father!
ALICE.   And all because he scorned her proffered hand.
EDG.   For my own mother! There! you've broached my all:
    O Mystery of this our being here!
    Had he accepted it, I had not been!
ALICE.   Not for her vengeance to descend upon.
EDG.   Her spite is past: she too is reconciled.
ALICE.   No: sooner shall the damned be raised to Heaven,
    Than you shall be admitted to her grace.
EDG.   But sure for Lucy's sake, if not my own.
ALICE.   Be undeceived: more brute than brutes, she is
    One of those hellowned mothers, who destroy—
    Oh! have me not to horrify your ear—
    Poor Lucy owes her birth and life to me!
EDG.   My preservation hallowed Lucy! Speak:
    Where is your pity, where your woman's heart,
    That you, who have been thus, can turn against
    The motherless?
ALICE.   Alas! my children both!
    I am not of the Fates, who spin the web;
    I can but teach you how to slip the meshes.
EDG.   O speak, my Oracle, my Prophetess!
    What shall I do?
ALICE.   See Lucy never more.
EDG.   Bid me keep from myself.
ALICE.   I charge you by that goal you hunger for:
    By your posthumous fame!
EDG.   It is a cheat:
    I'd have eternal fame, or I'd have none,
    And that no man shall own; no, there's no god,

Or fabled or revealed, whose credit stands
Five thousand years.

ALICE.   By Heav'n and Earth, and All that is between!

EDG.   The Universe is cleft atwain.
And wedges in my heart: there lies the out.

ALICE.   Then by your Mission and Eternity!

EDG·   Ha! now you rouse the echo in my soul,
Whose goad to action is the love of Man,
To me now sacred in the love of one!

ALICE.   Loved from your birth you must be loving still;
But oh! did you account your suffering?

EDG.   Account it? God! I feel it in the proof:
Humanity is still a heresy;
Yet I confidingly embrace the world,
But like that image of the Middle Age,
It strikes its secret daggers in my breast!

ALICE.   Though you be tortured, be adjured by me:
Oh! be not sacrificed!

EDG.   You bode of me,
As if I were a lamb in slaughterpen,
And must abide the drag-out and the blow?

ALICE.   My inner vision sickens to behold
What I may not portray. When you're engulfed
In that catastrophe you hazard now,
I'll be your herald to the other world.

EDG.   There are more awful moments in our life,
Than coming in, and going out of it,
And this is one. I must come to myself:
Alice, farewell!

ALICE.   Think, 'tis your mother lays
This hand upon your head: Oh heed me, heed!

EDG.   Through all eternity, but now I cannot:
Farewell, until we meet again. (going.)

ALICE.   (going to door.)   In spirit, but in body never more
(in door) Oh Edgar, take, oh take the other path!
Pay not the curse, wherein, the devil for
Their dower, holds the Ashtons in his pledge.
Mark well: before to-morrow's sun descends,
You'll have the earnest of my prophecy!

EDG.   Were it itself, I must go—there.

ALICE.   Oh would I were the despot of the world
For but one day!

EDG.   Ha! to what end?

ALICE.   To fetter you in adamantine chains,
Away from Lucy, her from you, and both
From your destruction!

EDG.   He who has willed the Despot and Destruction,
To quell their power, placed a stronger here.
By your own kindness be reminded nurse,
A loveless life, is at its best a curse.   *Exeunt.*

3*

SCENE II—*Mermaid's Well;* LUCY *seated on a rock, unleafs a dandelion.*

LUCY.   He loves me not—he loves—he loves me not:
Alas! I have but three more leaves, and dare
Not try it further: let me calculate
How they will end? Ah me! I'm so confused,
I cannot make it out, yet know I must. (*plucks again*)
He does—does not—he does! he does love me!
Oh sweetest, only flower of Paradise (*kisses it*)
Could you but take these lips, and tell me so!
Alas! How fond am I? How fond of all
The world, I fancy as his confidant!
There is no tree, no rock, I do not question,
And still the answer comes but from my heart:
I feel, I know, because I love him so,
That he must love me too: And yet, poor me!
Loved he—he would not stay! Can Alice then?
How drear it clouds before my eyes! My heart!
Though fear is bitter, hope is sweeter still!
My God, he comes! Ah now, how shall I act?
So dearly, sweetly would I have him know,
And yet I dare not tell! Kind Heaven, now
Let me find some mysterious avenue,
Besides my organs, to communicate
What heart intends to heart! Sure, he must see—

                Enter EDGAR.

I fear, that to the Master, Alice's hut
Has more attractions than the Mermaid's Well,
For fatal is this Spring to them, who come
To woo—its mermaids and its water-nymphs.
EDG.   So tells the legend of my ancestors,
But it does not relate, than any yet
Have rued the vision of an angel here,
For I'm the first so blest of all my kin.
LUCY.   Who were no kindred to those sons of God,
Who for its daughters visited this earth.
EDG.   For they are fairer than their mates above.
But sooth to say, I love this spot so well,
That if my disembodied Spirit may,
'Twill surely visit this Elysium,
For it was here I stocked my memory,
The garner of my soul, with such a store,
As gladdens her for all eternity,
LUCY.   Ah, then it was the person, not the place
That kept you hence?
EDG.   Since I felt reverence, I have worshipped Alice,
But knowing now, that she is intimate
With one, to me the dearest on the earth,
I love her second only to that one.
LUCY.   O sir, I am not cunning to construe,
Nor is it in my nature to presume,
Or take for granted what is unavouched—

EDG. (*aside*) How in our faults we are congenial!

LUCY. 'Tis true, I think, reflect and ruminate—
Oh sir, proceed : a half and doubtful tale
Were worse than none at all ; keep nothing back :
I feel, intensely feel, the time has come—

EDG. (*takes her hand*) Yea, it has come, and with a treasure
          fraught,
That tide of times shall never brag again.

LUCY. O Edgar, speak, speak on, and do not pause :
My bosom echoes what it dare not sound.

EDG. Yet listen Lucy : Alice told me all ;
That was the charm, that held me to her hut.

LUCY. O Heaven, true! I did betray myself!
What must you think of me ? Yet, God be thanked!
Now it is out, it has the breath of Life!

EDG. Amen, to that!
She warned me of this crisis in our life,
And I have passed it with a wary soul :
For he's a wretch, who will not meditate
Upon the consequences of his deed.
My dread alternative has been the choice
To never see you more, or front an ordeal—

LUCY (*Lays her hand on him, as detaining.*)
Oh do not leave—you shall not part from us,
Unless of me, you'll make a sacrifice.

EDG. (*takes other hand*) And of myself! Oh never dream,
          that I
Could quit where you abide, for on this earth,
There are more Edens, than what Adam lost.

LUCY. My Edgar! now my own, my only Edgar!
Fain would I tell you whence my love has sprung ;
How it has rooted, thrived and bloomed, how by
The blasts of doubt it has been wrenched and torn,
Till this blest moment it has ripened in
The calm assurance, that it is returned!

EDG. My own! amongst its thousand millions,
Kind Heaven lets the destined ones still find
Each other by its guide within.

LUCY. Oh, therefor be it ever thanked! In sooth,
I know not whether 'twas from gratitude,
For having saved my life, but since my eyes
Beheld you at this Well, 'twas only you
My soul has dwelt on in my thoughts and dreams.

EDG. And mine forgot all else, save Lucy's name ;
Oh! kindred are our souls, as were our hopes ;
And blest are we, who in this wilderness
Have found the voice responsive to our cry !

LUCY. The world is but an empty casket,
Till Love has set its gem. Oh, now this earth
Is Paradise again!

EDG. Yea, fair's this love apparelled world, and yet
In all this infinite of miracles,
The fairest is a woman in her prime,

And such, my Lucy, do I own in you,
The masterpiece of Heaven's wondrous hand!
LUCY.   Oh! Man, how I do love you!
EDG.   Yea, cling to me!
And 'gainst the world I'll hold you by this hoop,
Which binds the King and beggar still alike;
It is my mother's bridal ring; let it
Repeat its hallowed symbolship in you. (*puts it on.*)
LUCY.   My Edgar, mark the rare coincidence:
My owning this is since the birth of my
Young love for you: my father gave it me
The day you saved our lives, and bade me then
To give it him who should betroth my heart.
EDG.   If that were hap, then were the world by chance:
That dual day, on which was sown prodigious seed,
Whereof we harvest now.
LUCY.   And as to mine,
It yields this to your hand. (*puts it on his finger.*)
EDG.   Where 'twill avouch its truth,
If hence I doubt, that I but dreamt this bliss;
'Tis too angelic to affirm itself.
LUCY.   My ecstacy, being known alone in Heaven, earth
Affords no name to tell it by—
Could but the sweetness of this moment's spell
Dilate itself through all our coming time!
EDG.   My Love, we shall retain it through our life,
For Memory can lock the wheels of Time,
And let us revel where we now are rushed.
Come, Lucy, now we have each other won,
Let us devise how to secure ourselves
Against the Future. (*draws her to him on the rock.*)
LUCY.   My Edgar, fear not; all's as well, as 'twere
Already done. You have not only saved,
You have beatified my father's life.
He wills, and in advance has blest our bond.
EDG.   But so will not your mother. Lucy, heed:
If man was ever cautioned, I have been
'Gainst her remorseless hatred: she's the rock
We both must cross before we reach our haven.
LUCY.   Ah! Edgar! do not doubt, my father's will
Shall pilot us, so we may safely pass.
EDG.   Best to ourselves trust we our safety;
Then, if that warning should be verified,
Be you, for once her like in stubbornness,
But in all else remain still as you are.
LUCY.   Design me, Edgar, to what shape you will,
I am as wax to you. (*Moon rises.*)
                As I by you,
The ocean sways not by yon potent moon. (*Raven drops.*)
(*shrieks*) Oh! Edgar, see! What flutters on the ground?
How I am frightened! You are startled too!
Great Heaven grant, this be no augury!
EDG.   'Tis not propitious, and not ominous,
nd yet 'tis ill, in that it costs a life.

LUCY. Ah! see how pitiful he looks for help;
   Quick, draw the arrow, save him if you can.
EDG. It is too late : he is already dead.
   But this is singular and strange indeed ;
   The raven is the wariest bird, and none
   Have I yet known, who would abide the aim—
   And this so near as if to be our friend!
   But here his slayer comes.
          Enter HENRY *with a crossbow.*
HENRY.   That was a hit!
   Now, Master, think you, I can shoot a deer?
EDG. No doubt, you can ; but if you will persist
   To arrow all the ravens in the woods,
   You shall destroy the sponsors of our house.
   How would you like your own god-father killed?
HENRY. And if he were I still should keep my name.
EDG. So you care no more for your sponsor, than
   You do for mine? But can you answer for
   The deprivation of the raven's young?
   Who hence shall sate the callows' hungry throats?
HENRY. I'll find their nest—but as to feeding them?
   There, Lucy can provide for them: she is
   The foster-mother to all orphaned brutes.
EDG. Well, find them Henry: 'twill amend your fault,
   And to commemorate your archery, (*plucks some feathers*)
   I'll wear these feathers in my hat.
LUCY. And I will keep these blood-stains in my dress.
HENRY. Our mother brought you many nicer ones.
LUCY. Why, Henry, she has not returned?
HENRY. Be sure she has, and I am sent for you.
   She says, the news she brought, shall make you proud ;
   She's come to take you to the court.
LUCY. And, pray sir, what shall I do at the court?
HENRY. Why, court, and to be courted—bartered off ;
   For that, they say, are ladies taken there.
   All London is already on its knees,
   To compliment the Pride of Lammermoor.
LUCY. The Pride of Lammermoor?
HENRY. Ay, by that name all Windsor speaks of you,
   Who ought to thank that Captain Craigengelt
   For christ'ning you so lovely.
EDG. Ah! in our augury he's the evil bird.
   (*to* HENRY) But tell him, if in future he give names,
   My hand shall lesson him in sponsorship.
HENRY. I'll run ahead to say you're coming home.   *Exit.*
LUCY. I know him not, yet loathe him for his name.
EDG. And rightly, Love, your instinct counsels you ;
   These double tidings, paltry in themselves,
   Are in their combination ominous.
   And yet, were there no serpent in it, ours
   Would be no Paradise.
LUCY.   And be assured,
   That I shall profit by our mother Eve.

EDG. Heed but my words, and you are better warned.—
    You must to court?
LUCY. At Wolfe's Crag.
EDG. No, London, Love.
LUCY. As Lady Ravenswood.
EDG. Oh! you are mine, as I do own myself!
    Had Heav'n made you to my prayers, you
    Could not be better fitted to my soul,
    Who has forgotten all, save care for you:
    What most we prize, we still fear most to lose.
LUCY. I have one heart and troth for ill or good;
    There's but one Lucy and one Ravenswood.
                 Picture.

ACT IV.

SCENE FIRST.—*The Hall in Ravenswood Castle. Enter* ASHTON
and LADY; *she locks the door and takes the key.*

ASH. Why this precaution?
LADY. To teach a huckster in its sanctity,
    That I still prize a household's privacy.
    (*shows key*) Sir, let this warn you who is mistress here,
    The next time you presume to introduce
    Your daughter as the lady of the house.
ASH. A simple slip of tongue!
LADY. A sinister confession of your guilt;
    Your tongue did but anticipate the crime.
ASH. Of what?
LADY. The marriage of our daughter with this thing,
    That answers to the name of Ravenswood.
    The bankrupt whelp of our prostrated foe.
ASH. I can conceive the marriage—not the crime.
LADY. You would have learnt it in its punishment,
    But for my fortunate return.
ASH. Forsooth, we waited for your coming back.
LADY. To be accessory to your overt act
    Of treason to our house?
ASH. Before the fact, if you will have it so.
LADY. A vile untruth! You fain would have contrived
    My absence to a trap, in hope that then
    I would abide what could not be undone.
ASH. You have no proof of this.
LADY. Unless your ord'ring of the bans be it;
    'Tis sometimes well that Rumor has a tongue.
ASH. A villain's mouth owns this, who e'er it be.
LADY. 'Tis Captain Craigengelt: a worthy man.
ASH. A worthless knave: if you'll conspire with liars,
    You needs must be infected with their breath.
LADY. It is not so obnoxious as the man's
    In whom the father and the pander join.
ASH. This is too much; I have encouraged them,
    And when you know it all, you'll do so too:
    Abide this love awhile: see how 'twill fare.

LADY. Are you turned idiot thus to triffle with
    A thing you never knew: a woman's heart?
ASH. Then stay we neutral; Lucy shall decide.
LADY. I'd rather leave a serpent with a child,
    Then trust a moonish maiden with her heart;
    One sad experience is enough for me;
    Go and apprise this Ravenswood, we need
    His room for other visitors.
ASH. Are you possessed?
LADY.   Of such a firm resolve,
    As not your reas'ning shall disown me of.
ASH. What? I do that the savages disdain?
LADY. You prove that you are none by caring for
    The welfare of your family.
ASH. Whom you would damn with such a heinous sin,
    That Satan would disown our fellowship.
LADY. So do I Ravenswood; I rather brook
    A viper or a pest infected rag
    Within my house, than this forbidden man.
ASH. The savior of mine and Lucy's life!
LADY. Infatuated man! How do you know,
    But that you were the target for the ball,
    Which by miscarriage struck the bigger beast?
    I'd put it to the proof: what cause had he
    To come with gun upon another's ground?
ASH. How quick a heav'n can be perverted to
    A hell!
LADY. My lord, how will you? Nay, if you stay dumb,
    I'll take no answer for an answer too.
ASH. Propose whate'er alternative you will
    —As that, I drop the Master by degrees—
    I'll do it, but to bid him leave my house,
    Is what I will not, what I cannot do.
LADY. Sir, either he, or I shall quit the house;
    This my alternative; now take your choice.
ASH. In God's name then! If on my benefactor
    You will commit this infamy, I can
    Not hinder you beneath our common roof.
    But ere you do it, heed! A spot, that's once
    Defiled, invi es pollution to its end.
LADY. 'Tis you, who fouled it, by inviting him:
    Now see to it, that it be purged again.—
    You will not? Are not you the household's head?
ASH. You will not let me be it for our best,
    And so, I shall not be it for our worst.
LADY. Be then the vindication of our honor
    My task again, as it has ever been. (*sits down and writes.*)
ASH. What since our marriage have I never done
    I do it now! (*kneels*)
              My wife! my Margaret!
    Upon my knees I beg of you: desist!
    'Tis in my very heart you dip the point;
    'Tis with its blood you write!

LADY. So much the better: haply I shall drain
    Its vein of cowardice. (*unlocks the door and rings.*)
ASH. (*rises*) Be yours the blame; I wash my hands of this. *Exit*
LADY. Best lave them in your tears. (*sarcastically.*)

Enter SERVANT.

    Without a moment's loss, deliver this
    Unto the person known as Ravenswood.
SERV. Mean you the Master, Madam ?
LADY. The Keeper's master, anybody's master,
    Your master too, if you will have him so. *Exit* SERVANT.
    This check will warn him never to usurp
    The one prerogative I will not share:
    The mother who will let the father choose
    Her daughter's husband is an arrant fool.

Enter MARQUIS *with billet.*

    My lord, you come to broach no pleasant theme.
ATHOL. Then it is true, this is your hand ?
LADY.   And sir,
    It signed my mind. You speak, my lord, as if
    I would deny my deed ?
ATHOL.   Forsooth, I hope
    That by undoing, you'll disown your wrong.
LADY. There is no wrong, 'til we confess it such,
    And that I ne'er shall do.
ATHOL.   Your pardon, Lady,
    Had I known such to be your rule of action—
LADY. Methinks, you learnt it to your profit, for
    It sometimes makes an English Minister,
    To keep a rival from the Keepership.
ATHOL. (*bows*) I'll rest your debtor still, but for your anger !
    Come, Lady Ashton, for a son-in-law,
    You might look further, and fare worse, than with
    My nephew Ravenswood.
LADY.   So might my lord ;
    For if my gossips served me truly, he
    Is blest with marriageable daughters too.
ATHOL. I am no broker in my daughters' hands;
    I leave that to themselves and Lady Athol.
LADY. Aha, my lord! that is your Lady's business ?
    Then deign to leave the disposition of
    Her daughter's hand to Lady Ashton too—
    And let your kin shine in a Premier's beams,
    But in my house he lights not Hymen's torch.   *Exit.*
ATHOL. No; may he not, and may no other man !
    For in your hand, it is a brand from Hell,
    Though 'fore two angels to the altar borne.

Enter EDGAR.

EDG. If you are kin of mine, avoid this place,
    Unless you'll be contaminated with
    The shame that's cast on me.
ATHOL. I've tasted it, and may I get it's fill,
    If I stay longer, than to speak with you.

EDG.　This malice shames the fiend they learnt it from:
　　Not satisfied to rob this castle from
　　The father, but they here must gloat upon
　　The contumely of the beggared son!
ATHOL.　And being so, you should have kept away.
EDG.　O Sir! let him account why I am here.
　　Sir Ashton come, and kiss this hand again.
　　Once more, call me your son, and bring that bond,
　　You signed in blank; I'll fill it now with your
　　Commitment to the lowest depths of Hell!
ATHOL.　Oh! have no care; he'll not appear.
EDG.　I'm fain to think, God took him at his word,
　　And made him show without what he's within;
　　A monster of such black ingratitude,
　　That from his visage, Satan's self would stand
　　Aghast!
ATHOL.　Though she did perpetrate this infamy,
　　Yet shall Sir Ashton smart for it.
EDG.　You foul your tongue to name the shameful fraud,
　　Who got his manhood on a false pretense,
　　And now unmasks himself a woman's slave,
　　A damned, uxorious puppet of her whims.
　　Oh! that these shams, who backslide on their word,
　　Should be permitted by the upright world,
　　To prostitute the noble name of man!
ATHOL.　Enough of them; I'd now speak of yourself.
EDG.　Proceed: you have the ear of Ravenswood.
ATHOL.　You once disdained an offer I did make,
　　And bade me broach no charge in politics,
　　Save 'twere an honest service for the State:
　　I now have such a one.
EDG.　And have selected me, because I am
　　Your nephew? If you have, I'll none of it;
　　This nepotism is our country's curse.
ATHOL.　In you 'tis practiced in its utmost need,
　　For on the mission, I entrust you with,
　　To Germany, depend its peace and war.
EDG.　Oh! be it war! Chaotic war! And let
　　Its purifying thunder shake the world,
　　Until all placemen in the commonwealth,
　　Are settled by the standard of their worth.
ATHOL.　War in its season, but the country's mood
　　Now craves for peace.
EDG.　　　　　　　　Her palate shall be humored,
　　However the digestion foul her stomach.
ATHOL.　Then haste to start, for you must hence at once.
EDG.　Yea, verily I must! And how I must!
　　Yet, if the earth between us burst atwain,
　　I'll right me here, and if it end me not,
　　May then a whirlwind bear us from this den.
ATHOL.　She comes upon your wish: I yield my place;
　　Be wisely brief; we start together hence.　　　　*Exit.*
　　　　　Enter LUCY, *rushing into his arms.*

4

LUCY. My Edgar! Even this is possible!
    Oh! in this dreadful interval, I have
    Endured the doomsday's horrors of suspense;
    But now I have you, I am with the blest!
EDG. My Lucy, trust our mutual hearts with all;
    For what they once have drawn, they have the strength
    To hold for aye.
LUCY.   Then let us look on this
    As but a horrid dream.
EDG. We'd wrong ourselves if we did deem it more:
    It is the utterer of base coin that's shamed,
    Not he who throws it back.
LUCY.   Ignore it, Love!
EDG. Oh! heed it, Lucy, in our sense: it is
    That earnest Alice warned me of, and now
    It posts my nature with a giant's grasp
    To face the sequel's worse.
LUCY.   Oh! let it come!
    When I'm with you my sense of fear is dead.
    My Edgar, for my mother's hatred, sure,
    You do not love me less?
EDG. Were all the mothers in the world but yours,
    And were they worse than this, I'd love you all
    The more. The tiger-dam defends her young
    Against the sire; but hapless more than they,
    Your foes are your unnatural parents both.
LUCY. Oh! Edgar, had I been aware, she should
    Have ordered both of us, to quit the house.
EDG. And so she did, for Love, are we not one?
LUCY. Oh! true! With you, I too was bidden hence
    But do not go.
EDG. My Lucy, here I burn upon the stake;
    If I remain, I am consumed with spite,
    And if I go, my heart strings shall be cut,
    That tie me where you are.
LUCY. Oh! who shall part us? I will go with you
    To Wolfe's crag or to London, where you will.
               Enter MAID.
MAID. Miss Lucy, Lady Ashton bids you cease
    All conference with him, who's ordered hence.
LUCY. Tell her, that in this brunt, I shall receive
    No orders, save delivered by herself.   *Exit MAID.*
EDG. We shall go to the continent, to where
    I've entered on a public charge.
LUCY. The farther hence, the nearer to our home.
          Re-enter SERVANT, cautiously.
SERV. My Master, pardon me for warning you
    Against a violence, I cannot name,
    Not knowing of its like.
EDG. Say on: I deprecate her favor now
    More than her hate.
SERV. She means such execrable contumely,
    That all her men refused, whereon she hired
    Its executioners from the public road.

EDG. Thanks for your warning; wait my coming out.
Exit SERV.
    The sheer audacity of wickedness,
    Which needs but be confronted, and it shrinks
    Back to its nothingness.

LUCY. Whate'er befall, with you I'll share the worst.
    My Love, what will you do?

EDG. What shall I not do, in this love at bay?
    That Man alone is Man, who knows and does
    What every minute at his hand demands;
    But, Lucy, sooth, my prompter shall be this; (*kisses her.*)
    And if in action, I'm the least amiss
Enter CRAIGENGELT.
    Then let this devil start his imps to hiss.
    Sir, spare you tongue: I know the message from
    Its bearer.

CRAIG. Unless you'd squander the three-minutes, which
    The Lady grants you to leave Lucy and
    This Castle, you had better suffer me—

EDG. Will you avoid? (CRAIGENGELT *retreats up*)
    This ground is mined and Hell is underneath.

CRAIG. You wear a sword—some other time and place.

EDG. So, sir! (*turns him around and urges him to leave.*)

CRAIG. (*going*) Ha! I'll return this turn, if I must make
    A detour into Spain. (*sneaks off.*)

EDG.   What do I wait?
    But dupes will dream that Right asserts itself.
    Ha! now I read you motto of my house,—
    Five centuries are dropping off my soul,
    And here I've got my cue (*draws sword*) 'Tis not enough
    To save, but we must cause the loss of life,
    Ere in these juggling times we get our due.

LADY. (*without*) You craven hirelings, stand!
Re-enter ATHOL.

ATHOL. Sir, what a rashness! Only look without.

EDG. Do not believe, that I, who'd show the world,
    How to correct its wrongs, am at a loss
    To right myself.

ATHOL.   Trust me; through Parliament
    I'll wrest this castle from the Keeper's clutch.

EDG. And if you get it, keep it for your pains:
    'Tis not its loss, it's the wrong I grieve.
    He is but one; I'll be your precedent;
    Wrench you their spoils from all the public thieves,
    And in my heart, I'll set your monument.
    What, ho! A pass for Justice! (*leads out* LUCY.)

LADY. Tear Lucy from his side! Oh dastard dogs,
    Why do you yield? (*clashing of swords heard.*)
    (*shouts without*) A rescue! rescue, help!

ATHOL. If daring win, he's surely won his bride.   *Exit.*

SCENE II—*A Room in Girnintgon House; BUCKLAW and CRAIG-ENGELT sitting at a table; several bottles of wine before them.*

BUCK. True, Craigie, wine's a social creature in
    A twofold sense: we cannot lodge a bottle,
    It clamors for its fellow—let it come! (*hands him a bottle
        to open.*)
CRAIG. And mingle with the kindred spirits here.
BUCK. I hate an only bottle, and for lack
    Of better company, you'll do to save
    Me from that scandal—getting drunk alone.
CRAIG. My Lord, the B that follows on that A,
    Is—you consider me your parasite?
BUCK. As ever clung to forest tree.
CRAIG. If you construe our friendship thus—
BUCK. Our friendship? Pshaw!
CRAIG.   Then give me leave to say—
BUCK. What? You a captain? Where's your company?
CRAIG. Ha! ha!
BUCK.   Unless it be a coterie
    Of overkind and underloyal women,
    Whom you have under you! A captain? Pish!
    Why, you don't own a smack.
CRAIG. A thousand of them.
BUCK. I've never seen them.
CRAIG. You might have heard them, had you been but near.
BUCK. True; in your own report.
CRAIG. Sir, by their own: you do concede the women?
BUCK. The devil I do, sir: they concede themselves.
CRAIG. Well, then you'll grant, that I command their smacks?
BUCK. Ha! ha! Those are but smuggling smacks; yet sure—
    You're Captain there; but be my pilot here.
CRAIG. On all the seas of wine, you'll venture on.
BUCK. No, for this voyage, your peculiar one;
    So, watch this catch, and if you grapple it,
    You'll have fast hold on me for all your life.
CRAIG. That, Bucklaw, were indeed the hold for me,
    Who in this play of fast and loose with friends,
    Am now no longer trump.
BUCK. Well, hear to heed,—but fill the glasses first;
    Now pledge me to this toast: My future wife!
    But wherefore droops thy mighty spirit, and
    Why grow the rubies on thy cheeks so pale?
CRAIG. That *wife* has turned your wine to vinegar; ·
    Had you said *mistress*, 'twere a racy toast,
    In flavor and in favor both.
BUCK. How so?
CRAIG. Why, for the flavor of the thing itself,
    Then, by the time she'd cast me out, she'd have
    Outgrown your favor too—but, sir, a wife?
    Well, curse me, if I know the reason, why
    New married women so disrelish me.
BUCK. The longer wedded make amends for that.

CRAIG. Well, though they slight me on the whole, they like
　　Me for my parts; but devil take these brides;
　　They'll oust me ere the honeymoon has waned.
BUCK. Could you but stick, until that spell were past,
　　You might make good your pension for a year.
　　But come: I'll change your vinegar to nectar.
CRAIG. That were indeed a miracle.
BUCK. 　　　　　　　　Not at all;
　　'Tis but, that you provide me with a wife.
CRAIG. Ah! now I see; Oh! Fool! (*beats his head.*)
BUCK. 　　　　　　　You prove so now;
　　Why, Craigie, if you'd strike that numskull with
　　The hammer of St. Pauls's roaring Tom,
　　You could not rouse your wit: it drowses on
　　Too soft a couch.
CRAIG. (*rubs brow*) It's all along my curst farsightedness.
BUCK. Ha! ha! nearsightedness you'd say?
CRAIG. I mean it in the word's most daring sense;
　　Far off in India, yea America,
　　I sought my customer, and lo, behold! (*grasps his hand.*)
　　I have him to my hand, in Bucklaw here!
BUCK. I am your man, if she but answer me.
CRAIG. Oh! Man! what will you answer, when her looks
　　Shall rouse you as ne'er slogan did a clan?
　　(*kneels*) By Heavens! now, on bended knees I drink
　　Your toast of toasts: "Your future wife." (*They drink;
　　　he rises.*)
　　But you're to blame——
BUCK. For your foresightedness?
CRAIG. 　　　　　　　What else? You still
　　Would choose of women, as of venison:
　　You'd have them stale; the ranker their repute,
　　The more you relished them.
BUCK. 　　　　　　Well, those were slips,
　　But not the sort to be engrafted on
　　A family tree, and such a one I'd have.
CRAIG. In all the nurseries of the world, there's no
　　Such vig'rous 'scion, as the bride I know.
BUCK. Too rare, I fear, for me.
CRAIG. She's ready for your hand, as if she were
　　A new, uncalled for suit of clothes.
BUCK. Tell, who she is?
CRAIG. Miss Lucy Ashton.
BUCK. What? She, whose rescue from the Master, made
　　A gossip of the world?
CRAIG. 　　　　　　And well it might;
　　For that engagement broke the other up.
BUCK. How so?
CRAIG. Their marriage was frustrated by that fight.
BUCK. But is it true, it took a regiment
　　Of Cuirassiers, to capture her?
CRAIG. Had there been one horse less, they would have failed.

4*

BUCK. Indeed!

CRAIG. Most ignominiously; for Ravenswood
 Fought like a Nubian lion 'fore his den,
 And kept them still at bay, when they had closed
 Upon them in a circle; had there lacked
 A single link, they'd have slipt through the gap.

BUCK. So she was made a prize?

CRAIG. And how that regiment does prize its prize!
 Its battle flag, along those victories,
 In our rebellion, now blazons big
 The capture of the Bride of Lammermoor!

BUCK. Well, in the target of immortal fame,
 That last hits nearer than the others all.

CRAIG. Consider, what romantic savor streams
 From her, you'll have to wife?

BUCK. Ay, were it not, that she's forbidden fruit
 Though, being so, I'm tempted all the more.

CRAIG. O sir, be tempted still, until you pluck;
 A fruit she is indeed, as clustering and
 Exuberant in her charms, as were the grapes
 Here in their juice—but how is she forbid,
 When you're as welcome to her as to air?

BUCK. Ay, by her mother's, not her father's leave.

CRAIG. Know sir, in following that divine command
 To be one flesh, the wife's become the man.

BUCK. Though sure of them, I'm skeptical of the daughter,
 Who since her sundred plight, is said to be
 Indeed in wretched plight.

CRAIG. O Sir, to cure her contumacy, let
 The mother care, who better understands
 Her reins for breaking in a neckstiff girl,
 Than jockeys do their martingals for colts.

BUCK. Conceded—still, who weds a broken heart,
 Must mend it with his peace.

CRAIG. Remember, Lucy's of the Douglas stock,
 Who'd sooner break their promise than their heart.
 I'll vouch, that she'll as gladly mate with you,
 As she was loth to part from Ravenswood.

BUCK. When woman to man's plea accords her yea,
 Let him still know the reason why she yields.

CRAIG. She needs must cast a beggar for a lord.

BUCK. But he's a devilish deal the prettier man.

CRAIG. Who? He? Why he is swarthier than a crow,
 And for his size? well, grant him to be tall;
 But, sir, give me a light, stout, middle-sized—

BUCK. The plague upon you! You would say as much,
 If I were hunchbacked, halt and undergrown.

CRAIG. What matter, if you were? The mother will
 Convince her daughter, that this Ravenswood
 Is but a sorry dog, compared to you,
 The paragon of men.

BUCK.   And dupe of women!

CRAIG. You shall requite them by this marriage, which
 Shall aggrandize you both in wealth and honor.

BUCK. Where Interest points the way, we find conviction,
　　Without an argument; yet, spectre like,
　　A something warns me not to pick it up.
CRAIG. What? leave it lying for the next, that comes?
BUCK. Am I a coward?
CRAIG. Ha? That another than yourself shall doubt!
　　In courage, you're a nonesuch, braver than
　　Yourself—in drink!
BUCK. And yet, I may not cross the Master.
CRAIG. You shall cross after him.
BUCK. I have a dread, that if I counter him,
　　The penalty shall be this life he spared.
CRAIG. Pshaw! come, by sheer bad luck you slipt your sword.
BUCK. If this Miss Ashton were the devil's gage,
　　Instead of his, I'd dare the taking up.
CRAIG. I swear, she'll be the Grand Turk's thousandth wife,
　　Ere Ravenswood, who's worse than dead for her.
BUCK. Well then, she shall be, since she must be mine.
CRAIG. By heavens, now I'm so rejoiced in you,
　　I'd kiss you for it—if you were a woman.
　　(aside) Now I'm secure, the world may vex my like!
BUCK. But in the making of this match, how do
　　You stand accredited?
CRAIG.　　　　　　　Accredited?
　　Pish! on all credit! It's a cash transaction;
　　Delivery on the spot; demand her when you will,
　　And she'll be handed over.
BUCK.　　　　　　　Well,
　　I trust this business all in all to you;
　　Meet me to-morrow at the Notary's,
　　To write the jointure and the settlement.
　　But fill the bumpers; only in this sip,
　　Is there no slip between the cup and lip!
CRAIG. Here's to the pair, you next shall revel in. (they drink)
　　Now, Bucklaw, don't unbuckle, la!
BUCK. I am so full of wine and joy, I must
　　Let out my belt.
CRAIG. But don't let out your purse!
BUCK. Now, that reminder comes most apropos;
　　Here is to pay expenses. (throws him his purse.)
CRAIG.　　　　　　　Nay, Bucklaw, now
　　Upon my soul of troth, you use me ill—
　　Well, if you force me, I must needs submit;
　　I'd pocket an insult as lief as this. (pockets it.)
BUCK. Yea, do it meekly, without murmuring.
CRAIG. Ah, Bucklaw, you're a perfect god in drink;
　　I'm sure, that Bucklaw is the scotch for Bachus?
BUCK. Well, Venus changed her lovers every day;
　　Still Bachus would remain her favorite,
　　And therefore, Craigy,—hic—fill up again!
CRAIG. Thus we, who love to drink, now drink to love, (they
　　And hark ye, if upon your wedding day,　　　　　[drink)
　　Your courage fail, Oh be pot-valiant then!
BUCK. How so?

CRAIG. Why, for the natural, substitute
    The artificial valor—this.
BUCK.   May mischance overtake me, but I'll do it;
    I'll wed her—sober, if I can—drunk, if
    I must—thus recklessly oblivious
    I'd mate the daughter of the devil's dam.
    Step down the cellar—hic—and fetch us up
    A bottle of that sixteen, seventy-three. (CRAIG. *starts*.)
    Say, Craigie, now, if all the world were Spanish,
    You'd be—hic—general, and no tapster—eh!
CRAIG. For that I'll mulct you in a bottle more.
BUCK.   Well, let it be a dozen—hic —egad—
    Upon such news, we'll make a night of—hic—
        (*As* CRAIGENGELT *goes out,* BUCKLAW *tumbles off his chair.*)

ACT V.

SCENE FIRST—*The Hall in Ravenswood Castle; enter* LADY
    ASHTON *and* MAID *from opposite sides.*

LADY.   Your looks betoken (MAID *shows ring*) Give it me!
MAID.   I slipt it from her finger while she swooned. (*hands it.*)
LADY.   No matter for her swoons— Your destiny
    Was figured in your form; Your serpent's curse,
    In your refusal to my maiden hand.
    I'd have deserved, did I permit you to
    Repeat it on my daughter's. Though you slime
    My memory, you shall not hiss my hopes,
    For thus I bruise your head! (*puts it in purse.*)
    If you are questioned, you know nothing.
MAID.   Here is a letter too, the postman left. (*hands it.*)
LADY.   Again from Ravenswood! And you for him
    Gave one from Lucy?
MAID.   No, your Grace, not I.
LADY.   Beware! (*reads*) "The following post brings me to you,
    "Till then I am as one interred alive.
    "Your ever faithful, never changing Edgar."
    Go too, your predecessors' way: (*burns it*) Thus turn
    Their hopes to ashes! This betrayal proves
·   Th' improvident fool he is— Forewarned, forearmed.
    A fortnight hence, or in a week he's here,
    But I'll forestall him, if he come to-morrow;
    If she'll not bend, she'll break! Go tell your ward,
    Her respite is revoked: she must comply forthwith.
                                        Exit MAID.
            Enter SERVANT.
SERV.   Captain Craigengelt.
LADY.   Bid him come in.   *Exit* SERV.
    He comes upon my wish.
            Enter CRAIGENGELT.
                With all the haste
    You can command, bid Bucklaw to prepare
    His marriage with my daughter for to-night.

CRAIG.   This very night?   Now, this is news indeed!
LADY.   You well may say so, for it also ends
   The term of your probation.
CRAIG.   (*kisses her hand*)   Ah! your Grace!
LADY.   When in a son-in-law, I am secure,
   I may relieve me of my wedded clog.
CRAIG.   The sweet fruition of my hopes at last!
   But Urgency chokes dallying ceremony;
   I'll speed upon the lightning from your eyes.   *Exit.*
LADY.   Oh! what a difference 'tween man and man!
Enter BIDE-THE-BENT.
   Though loth, yet Reverend Bide-the-Bent, we may
   Abide your bending of our daughter's mind
   For only this one day—
BIDE.   Alas! your Grace!
   Then, in my person you dispense with grace?
   Must my preferment come to naught again?
LADY.   If you but will, you'll get its fill.
BIDE.   Ah, if your grace but wills it.
LADY.   Though with a high hand we might carry it,
   Yet policy forbids—
BIDE.   Wherein your Grace
   Approves herself a very Douglas still.
LADY.   If, for this last, your persuasion fail,
   Will you accord the holy sanction of
   Your countenance, however ruthless we
   Proceed with this undutiful daughter?
BIDE.   Why, bless your Grace, it is my avocation
   To go about, and spread a good report
   Of heaven's Lord,—Alas! he heeds me not,
   For I'm still unpreferred!—and shall I then
   Deny your Grace, who proves my better patron?
LADY.   (*gives hand*)   Sir, we're agreed—to save my perilled
   house,
   I'd rather shun a blunder than a crime.
BIDE.   There, still your Grace is wisely politic;
   Our Church has absolution for a crime,
   But for a blunder there is no relief.
LADY.   Well, reverend Bide-the-Bent, abide this night,
   And Scotland's richest benefice is yours.
   Here come our straying sheep: she has been once
   Our Shepherdess of Lammermoor, but now—
Enter LUCY.
   Your last spiritual guide you slandered as
   A bireling hag of hell, so now you have
   A Minister of Heaven.
LUCY.   His deeds, good mother, rather than your words,
   Shall teach us whence he hails.
BIDE.   Well said my daughter.
LUCY.   Would I were daughtered less, and fathered more!
BIDE.   Nay, in his servant shall you praise the Lord.
LUCY.   Oh! prove yourself a heavenly minister,
   By doing now its charity; counsel you
   My mother here, that she no further urge

Me be a traitress to my troth and soul;
Admonish her, how vile a deed it is,
To force a daughter to commit the sin
Of spiritual adultery!
BIDE.   How mean you this? You are not married yet?
LUCY.   Oh, sir, I am: here is my bridal ring—
Oh, Heavens! Mother! even this?
BIDE.   Ay, some Miss Ashton gave a rendezvous—
But 'twas not you—
LUCY.   Sir, you a reverend?
BIDE.   At Mermaid's Well, to Edgar Ravenswood;
That was no marriage; heath'nish were the rites—
The Lord who witnessed it, forgive the slip!—
'Twas all without the sanction of the Church,
Hence Heaven knows it not.
LUCY.   Oh, sure it does, for I'm in Heaven since.
But as you reverends have not tied our bond,
So you'll not losen it.
LADY.   But I command,
It shall be sundered!
BIDE.   Mark it well, your Grace;
To win his children from the Lord, the Arch-
Seducer weans them from his servants first.
Let us not hope, she doubts the scriptures too;
No vow, the parents disallow, shall bind.
LADY.   Therefor are men so faithless to their wives.
LUCY.   (to BIDE) Forbear; I thank my God, that he has
placed
Within, what prompts me know Him better, than
By His professing ministers.
BIDE.   Ha! if not
The hope of Heaven, nor the fear of Hell,
Yet shall you heed the terrors of the earth!
Hence be exhorted unto righteousness;
For, truly, you are to be pitied.
LUCY.   I were indeed, did I permit myself,
To be thus juggled of my troth and bliss—
Is it for this you would be praised?
BIDE.   Herein I needs must take your mother's part:
When you are Lady Bucklaw—
LUCY.   Sir?
BIDE.   I'll do
The same for you against your froward daughter.
LUCY.   Wherefor I'll pay you with—a benefice.
Pray, let me hence, back to my prison cell;
A loathed person is the worst duress.
BIDE.   The evil may abide no godly man.
LADY.   I'll meet you in the parlor.—   Exit BIDE.
LUCY.   Oh! mother, let us speak from heart to heart,
And spare me hence these intermediaries.
LADY.   You have repulsed the last; this night shall make
You Bucklaw's wife.
LUCY.   O God! Is it then true,
That you would do me this?

LADY.   Conform yourself.
LUCY.   It must be dreadful, not to own a mother,
    But it is killing to have one, and not
    To know a mother's love!
LADY.   And yet,
    That mother has endured her child-bed throes;
    Has perilled her own life in giving yours!
    Because, I am no doating, maudlin fool,
    To fondle and caress you like an ape,
    I am, forsooth no mother! Ingrate dupe!
    Thank my repellant nature, you're not spoilt.
LUCY.   I have bewept the hapless orphan's lot,
    But now? Ah! me!
LADY.   You wish you were an orphan too?
LUCY.   May Heav'n forgive me, from my soul I do;
    For I'm more wretched in my mother, than
    An orphan.
LADY.   You are convicted! I'm too much to you,
    And to your father; but, beware you both!
LUCY.   (*grasps her hand*) My mother, I implore you, say not so!
    I love you, love you more, a thousand times,
    Than you will give me leave to prove.—
    'Midst all my sorrow, I have ne'er forgot,
    I can have but one mother on this earth!
LADY.   Nor can you duplicate a spouse.
LUCY!   For me one husband in one Ravenswood.
    Oh! let me have him! he shall love you too:
    He does not hate you now: yea, when you wronged
    Him so, He willed you not one word of ill;
    Then, mother, be to him, as he to you.
LADY.   Be he to me, as I to him, unchanged!
LUCY.   My mother, I conceive a happier life
    Than now is yours.
LADY.   And so do I.
LUCY.   Ah! you shall have it, if you share with me.
LADY.   So I intend: with you and—Bucklaw.
LUCY.   Impossible! I'll yield and fit myself
    To all, so you but let me have my love.
LADY.   Your love's the fabric of your fantasy;
    Erase from it the name of Ravenswood,
    Then substitute Lord Bucklaw's in his stead,
    And see! your fairy palace stays the same.
LUCY.   As well breathe in my corpse a second soul,
    As make my spirit own another love.
LADY.   At your age, love is like a magic puzzle:
    Double your score of years, and lo! another picture.
LUCY.   No, mother, your own heart disproves such change.
LADY.   Break off—no more—you shall be Bucklaw's wife!
LUCY.   (*kneels*) Oh mother! but one week's delay!
LADY.   You had it: 'tis revoked.
LUCY.   But till to-morrow!
LADY.   Were I disposer of eternity,
    You'd get not longer till to-night.

Lucy. Oh mother, ponder it! if this be spoilt,
　　You can give me no second life.
Lady.　Because, I cannot, I dispose it so,
　　This one prove not your curse.　　　　　*Exit.*
Lucy.　(*rises*) Lost! Castaway! Undone, by whence I am!
　　Oh God! my sorrow is of huger size,
　　Than I can realize; but this I feel:
　　I'll not be Bucklaw's wife, and come the worst!—
　　The worst? Ah, me! what else but that can come?
　　My cheated hopes have gasped themselves to death!
　　The postman called and left—no line for me;
　　No Edgar comes to free me from my doom;
　　And my good Angel, I so fondly hoped,
　　Would succor me, in this, my utmost need,
　　Stays absent too: It is delusion all,
　　And I despair!
　　　　　Enter Henry *with Case and Willow-twig.*
　　My Harry still I greet you with a kiss;
　　Oh, take this from my soul, as 'twere my last! (*kisses him*)
Henry.　How is it with you, Luce? Your lips are ashy as
　　This willow, Douglas bade me bring to you.
Lucy.　His fittest gift, although he knows it not.
Henry.　He'd have me lie to you, the Master's bride
　　In Germany had sent it you to wear;
　　But sooth, I cut it at the Mermaid's Well.
Lucy.　Preserve it Harry; it will keep alive
　　Until you plant it on your sister's grave,
　　Where think, you read the saddest tale of love,
　　That ever thrilled and throed a maiden's breast.
Henry.　No, I'll replace it in its home, the Well.
Lucy.　And so you shall, for there I will be buried.
Henry.　That spot is dear to you—and by my troth!
　　This is the very dress, you wore that day,
　　I shot the raven there! You seem as fond
　　Of it, as I of my first kilt; and see!
　　Here are those blood stains yet.
Lucy.　O, then it bounded in a heaven!—Now,
　　It prisons in a drear, chaotic night,
　　Where starlike glitter but the thoughts and things,
　　My Memory elicits from that day:
　　All its associates, sorrow consecrates
　　To relics, and the dearest is yourself.
Henry.　I now like Bucklaw's present less.
Lucy.　That name forbid your lips: you took the bribe?
Henry.　You'll prize it better by your sight, than by
　　My praise: it is a dagger (*takes it out of case*)
Lucy.　The gift portrays the giver: a dagger to a child!
Henry.　A sword's too big: I wear it, dressed in state
　　Upon your wedding.
Lucy.　Ha, let me see it! Is it sharp? (*he hands it her.*)
Henry.　Damascus blade; its very shadow cuts
　　A hair; see but the inlaid pearl and gold!

LUCY.   I've shuddered to behold base, murd'rous steel
    So jewel honored ; now I feel its charm.
    I shall admire it, when I see't again   (*returns it.*)
    You'll wear it, are you sure, to-night ?
HENRY.   I shall,
    And go to dress me now ; you better haste,
    And do the same ; the sun sinks down apace.   *Exit.*
LUCY.   He goes, and with despair I'm left alone.
    (*kneels*) My heavenly Father ! In this final strait,
    My parents force me, I appeal to you ;
    For Earth affords no refuge to my soul,
    Whose only choice—the madhouse or the grave !
    If ruined Spirits still be fit for bliss,
    Oh, then let my firm resolution fail !
    But if amongst your blest, you'd have no soul,
    Save in its wholesome state, oh Father ! then
    Confirm my purpose, that I rush to you,
    Before that crazing storm undoes my mind,
    And prostrate, I'll account to you a life,
    Fraught with such sorrow.—Oh, my heart ! My brain !
    My father, save ! Oh save me ! Let me not go mad !
                                (*swoons.*)

SCENE II—*The Cabinet in Ravenswood Castle ; Enter* ASHTON,
                LADY *and* DOUGLAS.

ASH.   An evil air pervades our house : yet on
    The eve of the event, we may recede.
DOUG.   Shall I stand as a fool for Parliament ;
    And be defeated, but for Bucklaw's help ?
LADY.   (*to* DOUG.) Cease to be Colonel too, and be, like him,
    The beggar as I married him.   (*to* ASH.) But, sir,
    We spurn your baseness, as we would a worm,
    Than which you have no more ambition.
ASH.   Oh Douglas, is it naught to you, that since
    I'm set to order with my self, the world
    Does run so smooth with me ?
LADY.   Why should it not, since your's the downward course ?
ASH.   Because I've paltered with the man, who proved
    More than my child !
DOUG.   And did he not ?
    To the exclusion of your first born son,
    He got this very castle, while you live !
ASH.   Sir Athol did it, and not Ravenswood,
    Whom I shall father yet !
LADY.   Sir, whose perdition did you imprecate,
    Else in his issue, you be cursed again ?
ASH.   That curse of hate I'll change to friendship's blessing.
LADY.   By being damned through him in your own blood ?
ASH.   I'm pledged to him by Heaven's retribution,
    Not only on myself, but on my house.
LADY.   You did it then without authority :
    Your vow commits not me.
    5

DOUG.   And neither me.
LADY.   Nor any of my house; yea, not a dog
        Shall stand within its danger.
ASH.   Save alone
        My daughter and my perjured self; Poor Lucy!
LADY.   Your love for her is of the kind which apes
        Have for their young: to strangle them in their
        Fond ignorance, as you would her with Ravenswood.
ASH.   In whom our Scotland owns the genius of the age!
LADY.   May Heaven keep forever from my house
        The curse of thriftless genius, whereof
        The owner dies a bankrupt in estate!
        For me the tact and talent to achieve
        The stubborn fact of power and of wealth!
ASH.   His mission's great success will get him both:
        Think of his fame!
LADY.   Ah, like a new disease:
        No tongue, but croaks his name!
ASH.   The world converted to his teaching, shall
        Redate its era from his birth!
LADY.   He shall not be my son-in-law, and if
        He were the second savior of mankind.
        My son, do you still wish this marriage?
DOUG.   First and last!
LADY.   Sir, this the verdict on your last appeal.
ASH.   'Tis meet a wretch succumb, who lacks the strength,
        To bear him up.
LADY.   Your fears are idle, as they ever were.
        But tune your spirit to the festal mood,
        And all is well. Come, husband, I'll deem this
        My second wedding, happier than my first.
ASH.   I would not, yet I needs must dread.
LADY.   That's for you lose the daughter in the bride.
ASH.   God grant, that be my worst of loss! But, oh!
        Disaster hastens with gigantic strides!   *Exeunt.*

LAST SCENE—*The Hall in Ravenswood Castle, lavishly decorated
    for the Wedding;* BUCKLAW, CRAIGENGELT, HENRY, BIDE-
    THE-BENT, LORDS *and* LADIES.

CRAIG. My noble Lords, let us congratulate
        My patron on this feast, which will be famed
        While marriage shall prevail. (*bows, all do likewise.*)
BUCK.   My merit's but the acting on a hint;
        The credit of conceiving it, is due
        To Captain Craigengelt.
LADIES. (*gather around Craig.*) What happy man!
CRAIG. Yea, when the world hears of this nuptial pomp,
        The wedded will ignore their marriage, and—
ALL.   Ha, ha!
CRAIG. They'll have it over, modelled after this.
                        Enter DOUGLAS.
DOUG.   Be welcome, brother, to the Douglas house.

BUCK. Sir, I fraternize with your kin, unto ·
   The tenth degree—my Captain Craigengelt.
DOUG. (*slightingly*) I've had the honor.
CRAIG. (*aside*) This is the ill of being known too well.
   (*to* DOUG) I say it loyally : compared to this,
   The marriage of the Queen, was but a wake.
DOUG. Our means allow it, sir.
CRAIG. (*aside*) Ha! doffed again ; but I will face it out.
Enter LADY ASHTON *with* LUCY *gorgeously arrayed, followed by*
                SIR ASHTON.

ALL. Ah!
CRAIG.   Lord Bucklaw, and his bride of Lammermoor!
LORDS. Lord Bucklaw, and his bride of Lammermoor!
CROWD (*outside*) Lord Bucklaw, and his bride of Lammermoor!
LUCY. Oh, thus the sacrificial lamb is cheered!
 · But I, unlike, am conscious of my doom!
BUCK. This great ovation's greater moiety
   Is yours, my bride.
LUCY. To have it, would destroy it—keep it all,
   And it shall live.
BUCK.   Nay, verily, I protest. (*about to take her hand.*)
LUCY. Forbear, your touch is poison!
LADY. What! Is this your promise?
LUCY. I will be quiet—if I can.
   Unlace my stays—a shroud oppresses me—
   Take off these trappings! Give! Oh, give me back
   My Mermaid dress! (*is supported to a sofa.*)
LADY. Is't thus you are a bride?
LUCY. Of death!
LADY.   Nay then—Most Reverend Bide-the Bent,
   We ask your blessing on the ceremony.
BIDE. (*prays*) You, who by Lords are graced the mightiest
      Lord,
   As we look up to you, look down on us :
   Oh, blest the issue of these holy rites,
   And bless this couple for all time! Amen.
ALL. Amen!
LUCY. (*to* BIDE.) Is not the soul immortal?
BIDE. It shall not know corruption.
LUCY. Yet you deny to it its choice of mate
   For that eternity!
BIDE. The Church's grace smiles on a parent's cheek.
LUCY. Dissembling Parson! ere to-morrow night,
   You'll be accused before your Maker.
BIDE.   Ha!
LADY. (*takes from bosom*) Here are the marriage articles ;
      It first
   Behoves the father—husband sign.
ASH. It swims before my eyes—where shall I write?
LADY. Right here.
ASH. This pen's a bar of lead. (*signs.*)
LADY. To me it is but what it is—a quill. (*signs.*)
   My son, you're next in law, though first in deed.
                      (DOUG. *signs.*)

Most Reverend Bide, will you unbend yourself?

BIDE.   May through my fingers flow the Lord's good grace!
(signs.)

LADY.   (<i>to</i> BUCK.) My very son, first you, then Lucy signs.

BUCK.   For such a prize? I'd sign for hundred like.   (<i>signs.</i>)

LADY.   Now, daughter dear, the pen's the magic wand,
That with one stroke turns all your ill to good,
And makes you be my child indeed.

LUCY.   Ay, madam, for this once, I'll be your like.

LADY.   Ah, that's my Lucy now!

LUCY.   In her own will:
This hand, its instrument, was never made
To be my soul's undoer—I'll not sign!

ALL.   She will not sign!

LADY.   My noble guests, be not amazed at this;
Our daughter suffers with a malady;
She'll have her lucid interval at twelve o'clock,
And then she'll yield.

1st LORD.   What! Is she lunatic?

LADY.   She's somewhat mad with love; but marriage is
A sovereign cure for that, and I prefer,
She rave before, than rue it afterwards.
(Refreshments served around.)

LADY.   Hist, Maid: one word in private.

LUCY.   Henry, come;
Your dress is disarranged (<i>abstracts his dagger, and
conceals it in her dress.</i>) So, now, 'tis well!

LADY.   (<i>to</i> MAID.) Heed you: the bridal chamber; on your
life
Do not mistake it!

MAID.   Miss Ashton, you're to sad.

LUCY.   The bridal mood's to weep, and why not mine?
Three periods are the crises in our life:
Our birth, our marriage and our death! The first
I've had, the second I shall skip, so but
The third and last remains for me!

MAID.   Come, take some rest.

LUCY.   Where is our god, there is our heaven; this
Were mine, were Edgar here; but lacking him,
It is my hell; let's quit it.   <i>Exit with</i> MAID.

LADY.   Begin the music, order for the dance! (<i>Guests arrange.</i>)
Your arm, son Bucklaw. (<i>Music plays; light turned on.</i>)
What's this? The portraits changed! Who dared this deed?
(Music ceases.)

1st LORD.   The Ravenswood's in th' Ashton's place!

2d LORD.   What base affront!

3d LORD.   What insult to our host!

BUCK.   There's treachery abroad! Unsheath your swords!
Let's meet whatever come!   [<i>He and Lords do so.</i>)

LADY.   Tear down the traitors!
Not yet, the living dare to brave us here,
And neither shall the dead. The music play,
(They sheath swords; a dirge played.)

And onward with the dance! (*to* BUCK.) Hear this! A dirge?
Stop! Hold! The players, all the world's suborned!
(*As the Music hushes, a spectre-like figure glides across.*)
SOME GUESTS. Ha!
OTHER GUESTS. Lo, there!
1ST LORD. The ghost of Alice!
2ND LORD.   'Tis herself.
DOUG. (*follows*) Detain her! Seize her! Let the gates be
    closed,
LADY. Lord Bucklaw, haste! look to your bride : here take
    The key; she's in the bridal Chamber. (BUCKLAW *exit*
                                               [*hastily.*)
DOUG. (*returning*) Be not dismayed; 'tis all along a crazy
    wench;
    A rubbish left us by the Ravenswoods.
LADY. (*to* BIDE.) Your blessing went to Hell; recall it quick,
    Before it plague us more.
BIDE. The Lord must needs—
LADY. More interruption! are the doors not locked?
    Son, Douglas, how is this?
                    Enter EDGAR *with* ATHOL.
ALL. Ha! Ravenswood!
DOUG. (*he and* LADY *block their way*) How dare you in our
            castle?
EDG. 'Tis yours or not, according to my welcome;
    I bring you peace.
LADY. The conjuror has sent his tricks before,
    And here he is himself; the charlatan!
EDG. What? still injurious words! Then, Uncle, mine
    Must be the taking, not the giving way.
CRAIG. (*sword in hand*) By Heaven! myself will stab him
            where he stands!
ASH. Stop, Captain; there's no volunteering here.
ATHOL. Sir, this for you. (*delivers order to* ASHTON.)
ASH. An order from the British Cabinet,
    To quit this castle on the instant of
    Its presentation! Ravenswood! how could
    You do me this? (*sinks into chair.*)
EDG. You shall not fail me twice.
ASH. All I surrender you; be Master here!
LADY. Oh! recreant Dastard, would you thus requite
    This vengeance of the Ravenswoods?
    (*to* EDG.) Sir, in the school of Hell you learnt to read
    Yon motto; You knew well to bide your time!
EDG. To save you in your own despite.
LADY. Not with our castle do you get our child.
    She is another's wife.
EDG. 'Tis false! she would not sign.
LADY.   Sign or not sign,
    She never shall be yours; your charm's disowned
    By her it bound: here take (*hands him the ring.*)
EDG.   Yourself you dupe;
    The ring that binds us has been wrought by Heaven—
    Ha! where is Lucy! Speak! where is my bride!

LADY.   She is secure.
EDG.   And Bucklaw absent too?
    It strikes my brain—a thunderbolt!
    Oh, Monster speak with all your hydra-tongues:
    Where is my bride?
LADY.   Beyond your reach.
EDG.   Then I'll assert my right!
    (DOUGLAS *and* LORDS *draw their swords. The latter, as
    favoring* EDGAR, *open the way for him.* CRAIGENGELT, *in
    dumb show, reminds them, they are not bound to him, but to
    the Ashtons, whereon they obstruct his passage, until addressed
    by* EDGAR, *when they open it as before.*)
    (*to* DOUG.)   Bar not my way; I will.   Are you the knave,
    Who'd go to Parliament across his sister's grave?
                            (DOUGLAS *partly yields.*)
LADY.   (*to* DOUG.) What! you a Colonel? Let me have your
        sword.   (DOUG. *lays hand on his shoulder.*)
EDG   By Heavens! Douglas, for your sister's sake,
    I love you better than myself—let go! (DOUG. *does so.*)
LADY.   Were you not from the surer side, I'd say,
    You are a bastard to the Douglas house.
DOUG.   (*to* EDG.) Go back, unless you'd step across their
        swords;
EDG.   Corruption glutted Lairds! Behold, to what
    Your country's sale has brought you! But be still
    The stirrup holders to the ruling Lords,
    Until the Commons shall confound you both!
LADY.   (*to* DOUG.) Are you infected by their cowardice?
DOUG.   His look benumbs me, mother.
EDG.   I'm but a drowning man and sink the third,
    Last time. My Lucy, Lucy, I am come!
LADY.   (*to* DOUG.) O pusillanimous slave! for what wear you
    A sword? (*about to grasp it.*)
DOUG.   Nay then; look, Master, there's my sister! (*stabs him
                            [in the side.*)
LADIES.   (*shriek*) Murder!   (*all rush out.*)
EDG.   (*is supported to seat.*) O Alice! Prophetess!
    Now do I know it, but to end it all!
    Oh! look for Lucy! now—I can—no more—
ATHOL.   (*to* DOUG.) I have a mind to send you back to Hell,
    You left a void, none but yourself can fill.
    (*to* LADY.) Make it your mother's boast, to own so old
    Assassin in so young a son!
LADY.   So old?
ATHOL.   As you, who did what all its men could not:
    You've damned the name of Douglas for all time.
                    Enter CALEB.
CAL.   Wolfe's Crag is struck by lightning.
EDG.   And in time. (*swoons*)
CAL.   (*supports him*) Alas! my Master!
ATHOL.   Lords guard the doors, and hold
    The two assassins with her paramour. (*Lords guard doors.*)
ASH.   Her paramour! Who? Captain Craigengelt?
ATHOL.   So says the world.

ASH.   Oh! serpent hag, is this
    Your second marriage, happier than the first ?
LADY. If you had been, not I had been the man.
ASH. For this was I a double dealing wretch !
    Live, Master, live ! Come I will bind your wound.
CAL. Not to a king I'll yield it. (*bandages him.*)
ASH. Revive and live for Lucy ! She is yours.
EDG. (*recovering*) Not me—save her—all else cut short—she'll be
    Undone ! search for her ! Rouse the house ! haste all !
ASH. Sir, she is well,
EDG. Oh ! why am I then murdered ?
ASH. (*to* LADY.)   Woman, where's
    My daughter ?
LADY. Where else, but with her bridegroom should she be ?
ASH. (*to* EDG.) You hear, she's safe.
EDG. Great God ! Are you unwitted all ?
ASH. True, I am curse benumbed.
EDG. Oh ! fly—search all the rooms ! (*general commotion.*)
HENRY. Where is my poniard ?
ASH. Now Heaven, spare that curse !
BUCK. (*within*) Help ! Murder ! Help !
EDG. Oh ! my presaging fears ! I'm murdered here ;
    She's slain within ; we die a double death !
BUCK. (*within*) Help ! save me ! Oh !
             Several MAIDS *rush in.*
LADY. Quick, Douglas ! To the Bridal Chamber.
               Exit DOUG. *into Chamber.*
    (*to* LORDS) Stay back ! let none but women enter. *Exeunt*
    ASHTON *and* MAIDS *into same.*
DOUG. (*returns to door*) O horror, horror ! Blood, how quick
    you bred,
    It is my murder, that's begotten this !
    I dare not back ; search you for her ; she's murdered him.
    (BUCKLAW *from another door is borne across the stage.*)
ASH. (*inside*) Oh ! my poor child !
EDG. (*to* CAL.) Now, do your dearest service, bear me up.
    (LUCY, *is borne in, followed by* ASHTON.)
ASH. (*breaks down*) My poor, curse stricken Lucy !
LUCY. He's come ! My bridegroom summoned me !
1ST MAID. You've murdered him.
EDG. (*sinks beside her*)   He lives to die with you !
LUCY. (*shrieks*) Ah, Edgar ! You're not hurt ? Not you I
    struck—
    Not you did wrench the terrible dagger from
    My hand, and plunge it here ! (*points to gash*)
EDG.   Oh ! God ! 'twas there,
    Not here, my life was struck !
LUCY. Oh ! had you come a minute sooner ; then !—
    But no lamenting now ! My life was but
    One wish, that you be mine, and now I'm blest ;
    What Life denied me, kinder Death allows ;
    My husband !

EDG.   For Eternity! Our bliss
     Being more than earth's, we could but taste in hope.
     Oh! we had strayed in the wrong mansion of
     Our Father's house, and this has been our fare!
LUCY. 'Tis not my wound it is my heart that breaks.
     My Edgar, since you saved my life, I walked
     But on a tether round the stake of death ;
     And when you joined me, life did glide so sweet,
     We wound it up too quickly. Pray live you,
     And let me die alone.
EDG.   Do not believe it!
     Between our souls the tackle is too strong,
     And neither snaps, but drags the other on ;
     Here is the rent of mine (*tears off bandage*) One life, one
          death!
LUCY. Our grave's bespoken at the Mermaid's Well. (*dies*)
EDG. In you, I loved mankind ; my spirit, in
     Its parting throes, would over at my eyes,
     That to their woes, it hence can throb no more.
ATHOL. Oh! you who ever pored on death, impart
     Us your presentiment.
EDG. I could put tongue into that lasting book,
     Whereof yon dial is the title page,
     If it were not, that my precursor tugs
     Me from this pivot of eternity!
     Let me see nature! (*window opened*) On my heart I bear
     Your mother-mole ; Oh! now take back your son! (*dies*)
CAL. (*holding one hand*) My Master!
ATHOL. (*holding other hand*) Oh! Ravenswood!
LADY ASHTON, DOUGLAS *and* CRAIGENGELT *are arrested as*

THE CURTAIN FALLS.

www.ingramcontent.com/pod-product-compliance
Lightning Source LLC
Chambersburg PA
CBHW030856260626
47169CB00008B/2561